From Spark to Story, Vol. 2
Tina Harden

Soriano Ragazzo Publishing

©Copyright

FROM SPARK TO STORY, Vol. 2: A Short Story Collection by Tina Harden © 2026 All rights reserved.

No part of this publication may be reproduced, distributed, or transmitted in any form or by any means, including photocopying, recording, or other electronic or mechanical methods, without the prior written permission of the publisher, except in the case of brief quotations embodied in critical reviews and certain other noncommercial uses permitted by copyright law.

For permission requests, write to the publisher at: Soriano Ragazzo Publishing, 2620 Clarke Dr, Lake Havasu City, AZ 86403, Email: sorianoragazzopublishing@outlook.com   Author contact: authortinaharden@outlook.com

ISBN: 9798898900120
LCCN: 2025924103
EPUB: 9798898900045
Large Print: 9798898900076
Complete Set Vols. 1-4 Hardback: 9798898900694

Disclaimer: From Spark to Story is a work of fiction. Names, characters, organizations, and incidents are products of the author's imagination or are used fictitiously.

References to recognizable public figures, institutions, or existing organizations are solely for creative or contextual purposes. Their appearance is not intended to suggest affiliation, endorsement, or factual representation of any real entity or program.

Cover and interior design by Soriano Ragazzo Publishing, Tina Harden. Published in Lake Havasu City.

Contents

Introduction	V
From Spark to Story	VII
The Winter of Our Discount Tent	1
The Morse Code Murders	7
Maritime Sand	13
Australian Vernacular Guide for 'The Tree and the Tarn'	21
The Tree and the Tarn	23
The Alchemist's Folly	53
Silent Famine	57
The Incident in Room 629	61
Revenge a la Frostbite	65
The Tides of Freedom	67
Pillars of Strength	73
The Frozen Smile of Lake Chautaugua	111
The City of Speakeasies in the Galaxy of Prohibitionia	113
The Passage to Eternity	125
The Snowmen of Tippah County	137
The Boy and the Sands of Al-Khayal	141

Dorian, the Ink Drinker	147
The Clicking Never Stops	155
Beneath the Waves	161
About the author	169
Also by Tina Harden	171

Introduction

IN THIS SECOND VOLUME of *From Spark to Story*, Tina Harden dives beneath the surface to explore the raw edges of survival, sacrifice, and the stubborn flicker of hope.

These longer, emotionally charged stories span continents and eras—from deserts scorched by cartel violence to the mist-wrapped highlands of Tasmania and the haunting depths beneath the sea. Within these pages, readers will encounter women who endure, men who reckon with their pasts, and spirits that refuse to fade.

Pillars of Strength tests the limits of courage and vengeance; *The Tree and the Tarn* roots legacy in love and loss; *Dorian the Ink Drinker* blurs the line between obsession and art; *The Passage to Eternity* delves into the unknown; *Beneath the Waves* reveals what lies in the heart of myth; and *Maritime Sand* confronts the price of progress.

Told with Harden's trademark mix of intensity, humanity, and cinematic detail, *From Spark to Story - Volume II* delivers a collection that lingers long after the final page.

From Spark to Story

THE FIRST VOLUME OF *From Spark to Story* is a sample of writing exercises I've used to limber up the writing muscle. Then there are flash fiction pieces—some enhanced from the writing exercises—the rest from prompts and writing requirements for critique group.

I am a member of Lake Havasu City Writers Group in Arizona. We meet each first and third Saturday of the months. We are tasked with writing a 250-word story to specific prompts the group selected.

The following stories—larger and grittier than Volume 1—are unseen, with exception of a couple, by the LHCWG.

A majority of the stories I've included started from a simple spark—whether from a joke I heard—or a nugget of historical fact. Hence the title I've chosen for my anthologies, From Spark to Story.

The Winter of Our Discount Tent

"Now is the winter of our discount tent," Marla declared, unfurling something that looked less like camping gear and more like something that resembled a nylon jellyfish having an existential crisis.

Dan crossed his arms. "Discount from what? The Titanic's lifeboats?"

"It was seventy percent off," she said proudly, shaking the limp fabric. "End-of-season clearance."

"Yeah, I can see why the season ended."

They stood in a barren, snow-dusted campground—the only souls optimistic enough to think camping in January was a good idea. Sage, their teenage daughter, sat in the car, scrolling on her phone even though there hadn't been a signal since the welcome sign.

Uncle Rick, a self-proclaimed outdoorsman and part-time philosopher, stomped into view carrying two mismatched tent poles. "Who needs directions? Real campers improvise!"

"Real campers," Dan muttered, "book hotels."

It took three adults and one near-divorce to raise the tent. When it finally stood, it leaned so badly it looked tipsy enough to need a sponsor. "Perfect," Marla said. "See? Family bonding!"

"Looks more like hostage negotiation," Dan replied.

***

Night fell early, wrapping the campground in a glacial hush. Their breath fogged inside the tent, where the so-called *thermal lining* felt suspiciously like tissue paper. Sage, swaddled in her sleeping bag, grumbled, "I can't feel my soul."

Rick tried lighting the camp stove. It coughed, flamed, and died in one melodramatic gasp. "That's all right," he said. "We'll rough it. I once cooked ramen using only body heat."

"Then please," Marla said, "keep your body heat away from my cocoa."

Dan poked at the stubborn fire pit. "You know, most families spend the holidays under a roof."

Marla shot him a look. "And miss this majestic view?" She gestured to the frozen lake, the silver sky, the occasional flake sneaking through the tent flap.

"Majestic's one word for hypothermia," he said.

***

By midnight one air mattress had deflated to a tragic pancake. The tent walls rippled in the wind, sounding like a thousand plastic grocery bags gossiping about their life choices.

Outside, a raccoon rifled through the cooler.

Sage mumbled, "Something's out there."

"Probably nature," Rick said.

Dan sat up, flashlight trembling. "Define nature."

The beam caught two glowing eyes. The raccoon hissed—indignant—and waddled off with half their trail mix, as if *they* had ruined *his* evening.

Marla sighed. "At least someone enjoyed dinner."

By morning, the world was white and silent. The tent had partially collapsed, burying Dan under what used to be the roof. Marla dug him out with a spatula—the flimsy kitchen kind.

"Don't say it," he groaned.

"I told you we should've brought the good spatula."

Rick was outside scraping ice off his mustache, humming something suspiciously heroic. Sage filmed everything on her phone, narrating for her imaginary followers: "Day two in the wilderness. Parents losing it. Uncle might be part yeti."

They huddled around the useless camp stove, passing around a thermos of lukewarm cocoa. The wind moaned through the trees like a distant complaint.

Marla's smile wobbled. "Okay, so it wasn't perfect. But we're surviving, aren't we?"

Dan raised an eyebrow. "Define surviving."

She looked at her family—half-frozen, under-caffeinated, and utterly miserable. And yet, somehow, still hers. The absurdity bubbled up in her chest until she laughed. "Next year," she said, wiping her eyes, "we're doing a discount cabin."

Rick nodded solemnly. "Or a luxury couch."

***

The park ranger found them an hour later, packing up a tent that now resembled a sad origami project done by a frostbitten child.

"Cold night, huh?" he said.

Marla beamed. "Not too bad! We're practically pioneers."

Dan muttered, "Pioneers died doing this."

The ranger chuckled. "You folks heading home?"

"Straight to civilization," Sage said. "With walls. And Wi-Fi."

As they drove away, the tent flapped in the back like a wounded flag of surrender. Snow sparkled on the road ahead.

Marla turned to Dan. "Okay, maybe it wasn't my best deal."

He smiled faintly. "You think?"

She grinned. "But you'll remember it forever, right?"

He sighed. "Every time I see frost, I'll hear your voice saying, 'Now is the winter of our discount tent.'"

She laughed. "See? Worth it."

Behind them, Uncle Rick waved from the back seat, holding a mug of cocoa like a victory trophy. Sage typed something into her phone:
Family trip: 2 stars. Would freeze again—only for social media content.

###

Writer's Choice, Humorous Fiction
*The spark for this is mis-heard song lyrics and play-on-words. It triggered several stories like this.

The Morse Code Murders

EMILY SAT IN HER dimly lit room, fingers pressed to her temples, the familiar hum of tinnitus crawling like static through her skull. It had been years since she first noticed it. At first, just a faint buzz. Now, a constant, maddening companion.

Tonight, she logged into the virtual chat support group, a rare safe haven for fellow sufferers. Her friend Johnny popped up shortly after—they'd met here, bonded over shared frustrations, late-night worries, and the absurd humor that sometimes helped them cope.

But tonight felt off. The air felt charged, like a storm waiting to crack.

"Hey, Johnny," she typed, fingers hovering. "Do you feel weird tonight?"

"Yeah. Something's... off," came his reply.

As the group trickled in, the usual small talk faded. That's when it started: sharp, irregular clicks threaded through the background static. Emily froze, heart thudding.

"Anyone else hearing that?" she asked.

"Definitely," Jenna chimed in. Her usual sarcasm was gone, replaced by something tight and uneasy. "It's like... Morse code or something."

For a beat, nobody typed.

Emily's chest tightened. She'd always thought her tinnitus was worse — different — from others'. She used to joke it was trying to "say something" when the patterns shifted. But tonight, it wasn't funny.

One by one, group members spoke up, describing the clicks they'd been hearing. Different tones, same desperate rhythm.

"Wait," Johnny wrote. "I'm getting something... S-O-S... H-E-L-P... M-U-R-D-E-R."

Emily's mouth went dry. She stared at the screen, pulse drumming in her throat. "Are we... are we hearing ghosts?"

The chat exploded. Disbelief. Nervous jokes. Raw fear. But underneath it all was something magnetic: the pull of the unknown.

They worked together, decoding fragments. Names. Dates. Places. Jenna pulled up news articles, Johnny cross-checked social media, and Emily's brain raced to connect dots. That's when they saw it — the victims were all tagged at the same annual music festival days before their deaths.

Emily swallowed hard. "The festival's in a few weeks."

Jenna hesitated. "Do we... do something? What if this is just our brains messing with us?"

"We can't ignore this," Emily typed, fingers trembling. "If they're reaching out, we have to listen. And if we're wrong... at least we tried."

A pact formed, fragile but determined. They exchanged numbers, mapped out clues, and agreed to meet.

For the first time, Emily's tinnitus felt like a gift, not a curse. It was pointing her toward something.

***

The day of the festival arrived in a haze of nerves and adrenaline. Crowds surged. Music pulsed. Emily and Johnny moved through the chaos, the clicks in their heads louder now, almost guiding them.

Then, it happened.

Emily stopped cold. A face — familiar, impossible. A young woman, bright smile, eyes like she remembered from the news. But no, she was gone.

The clicks turned sharp, urgent.

Find him... the man with the guitar...

Emily gasped. "Johnny," she choked, "he's here."

Johnny spun, scanning the crowd. "Who?!"

They shoved through, following the invisible thread. Near a food booth, they spotted him — a man with a guitar, casually strumming.

Emily's skin prickled. The melody — it was the same song playing in her head. This wasn't random. This was the sign.

Heart hammering, they approached.

The man looked up, frowning. "Can I help you?"

Johnny's voice shook. "You killed them."

Panic flickered across the man's face. "What are you—no—you don't understand—"

The crowd sensed the shift. Heads turned. Phones lifted. A security guard nearby spoke into his radio, eyes narrowing. And behind it all, Emily felt them — the victims — pressing at her back, pushing her forward.

Suddenly, sirens blared. Police burst through. The man bolted, but it was too late. They tackled him to the ground as the crowd erupted in confusion and whispers.

***

At the station Emily explained to Detective Samuels how the faint clicks in her ear tapped out a rhythm no one else heard. She'd traced the pattern for weeks — short, long, short — until the Morse code cracked open a name. Mick Hale. The guitarist from the corner bar, the one who played like the strings were veins and he was cutting through them.

Detective Samuels hadn't believed her at first. "Tinnitus doesn't spell out killers, Emily." But here they were, in the station, the smell of old coffee and cold sweat in the air, staring at the man who'd haunted her static-laced nights.

Mick sat cuffed under buzzing fluorescents, fingers twitching like they still held a pick. Samuels paced, shoes scraping linoleum, every step dragging across Mick's nerves.

"You killed them because they were loud? That's your reason?"

Mick smiled, calm, almost serene. "You ever have static in your head, Detective? Constant, ceaseless? You start craving silence like a man dying of thirst craves water."

Samuels scoffed, but Mick barely heard. The clicks were back. Short, long, short. It had started after Derek, the drummer, overdosed. That night the band played too hard, too loud. The ringing never left. And then came the messages.

Cut the noise.
Still the chaos.
Quiet, quiet, quiet.

At first, the guitar drowned them out. But after every show, the whispers returned, sharper, needling his brain. His hands ached, not for music, but for stillness.

Samuels leaned in. "So you became a killer."

Mick let out a soft, almost childlike laugh. "No," he murmured, eyes glinting under the harsh lights. "I became the silence." Closing his eyes, he smiled faintly, as the clicks in his head spelled one final word: *More.*

Emily shivered, the sound still tapping against her eardrum, and wondered if the music in her head would ever stop.

***

When the dust settled, Emily and Johnny stood side by side, shaking, breathless. And then, the strangest thing.

The clicks stopped.

Not gone. Not forever. But quiet — replaced by the familiar, almost comforting hum of tinnitus.

Emily exhaled, a tear sliding down her cheek. She hadn't just heard the dead. She'd helped them.

And for the first time in years, the noise in her head wasn't just noise.

It was a connection.

A purpose.

###

Speculative Fiction

*The spark for this story came from my lifelong tinnitus that recently changed to an annoying *clicking* in my left ear—sounding like Morse Code.

Maritime Sand

The waves of the Pacific Ocean lapped gently against the shore of Bondi Beach, their rhythmic dance a soothing backdrop to the early morning joggers.

In the distance, the Sydney skyline stood tall, a collection of steel and glass giants reaching for the sky. The salty breeze carried a hint of something new, a faint scent of promise mixed with the familiar brine.

Above the horizon, a solitary ship cut through the water, its silhouette a stark contrast against the rising sun. It was the S.S. Meridian, a sand carrier that had become a regular sight in these waters.

A precious cargo filled the ship's hull, soon to be swallowed by the insatiable hunger of distant lands.

In a bustling office in downtown Sydney, Mark, a seasoned marine biologist, sat hunched over his desk, surrounded by maps and charts. His eyes scanned the latest sonar readings, tracing the contours of the ocean floor.

The fine grains of silica sand, invisible to the naked eye, were the focus of his intense gaze. His job was to locate and secure the future of the city's construction industry, one grain at a time.

Yet his mind was not fully on the task. His phone's lock screen displayed a photo of his children building sandcastles on the beach.

Previously, their cheerful faces had comforted him, but now they felt like a cruel mockery. He had built those castles on sand dredged from the same ocean he'd sworn to protect.

The phone on his desk buzzed, breaking his thoughts. "Mark speaking," he answered, already expecting the worst.

"It's the Marine Exporters Association," the voice said. "Mark, Saudi Arabia's order just came in," the voice crackled. "Biggest shipment yet. Two weeks to load."

Mark's pen hovered over the chart. "That's pushing our limits."

"Limits don't matter to the client, Mark."

Mark scribbled furiously, his grip tightening on the pen. The seabed was close to its limit, and this order can push it over the edge. Glancing at the family photo again, a knot formed in his stomach. *What kind of world was he helping to create for them?*

After hanging up, Mark headed to the conference room, where his team waited. The room was abuzz with conversation, but one voice stood out: Emily, the young intern. Her passion often outpaced her experience, but Mark admired her drive.

"Saudi Arabia's placed another order—biggest one yet. The S.S. Meridian needs to load up and head out within two weeks."

"This is unsustainable," Emily said, her voice tinged with frustration. "We need alternatives."

Mark raised a hand, silencing the room. "I agree, but the government won't let us stall. If we don't find a deposit, someone else will—and they won't care about the reef."

The room was thick with tension, but Mark remained calm. "We'll need to survey the area off Newcastle," he said, pointing at the map. Although the water is deeper, less sediment movement means a more stable sand bottom.

The team nodded in agreement, and the room buzzed with the sound of strategizing. They had to move fast. To meet the Meridian's departure deadline, they required accessible, high-quality sand. Emily frowned but said nothing. Her disappointment lingered in the air, a silent challenge.

Out on the water, the S.S. Meridian's captain, Tom, leaned against the rail, watching the waves. He'd sailed these routes for decades, witnessing the slow erosion of the ocean's riches. The image of a Southeast Asia reef, once teeming with life, now desolate after years of dredging, haunted him.

As the ship approached Newcastle, Tom radioed the bridge. "Keep an eye out for the survey boat," he said. "And watch the current—it's stronger than usual near the drop-off."

They deployed the survey boat, and Mark's team descended into the depths of the ocean. The underwater world was alien, silent, and majestic.

Schools of fish flitted by, and the sun's rays pierced the water in shimmering beams. The submersible's lights illuminated the seabed, revealing a landscape of undulating dunes and ancient rock formations.

His first mate chuckled. "You worry too much, Captain."

Tom didn't respond. Worry had kept him alive this long, and he wasn't about to stop now.

Mark's team worked tirelessly, collecting samples and mapping the seabed. With every grain they sifted, every sample they took, the team had an acute awareness of the responsibility they held in their hands.

While the extracted sand will fuel the growth of cities half a world away, dredging will leave a never-healing scar on the ocean floor. They worked meticulously, taking care not to disturb the marine life that had made this place their home.

Emily's excitement was palpable as she operated the sonar equipment. "This spot's promising," she said, pointing at a cluster of dunes on the monitor. "The sand's fine, and the reef's farther out than we thought."

Mark studied the data but hesitated. The area was teeming with seagrass beds, vital to marine life. "We'll document it," he said, "but let's keep looking."

Emily slammed her hand on the map. "We're destroying the seabed faster than it can heal."

Mark met her gaze. "And if we don't extract, someone else will—someone who—they'll destroy everything."

"So we're just supposed to accept—"

"No," Mark cut her off. "We're supposed to be smarter."

Emily was unconvinced, but nodded. "There has to be a better way."

As the survey continued, Mark wrestled with doubt. The data confirmed the site at Newcastle meets the order, but at what cost? Every grain they took felt like a betrayal of his principles.

After the meeting he called his wife. "How's the soccer game?" Mark asked, forcing lightness into his voice.

His wife's tone was tired. "The kids keep asking when you're coming home."

A pause. "Soon," he promised, knowing it was another empty commitment.

After hanging up, he stared at the framed photo on his desk. *What kind of father am I if I can't leave them a healthy world?*

***

Back in Sydney, Mark presented his findings to a panel of government officials and environmentalists. The room was tense, the stakes higher than ever.

"We've identified a site," Mark began, "but it's with a fresh approach: sustainable extraction combined with restoration. It's slower and costlier, but it's the only way to protect the reef."

The officials exchanged skeptical glances. A stern-faced official leaned forward. "Guarantee results?"

Mark didn't flinch. "I can't guarantee success. But I can guarantee that doing nothing will definitely fail."

After a long silence, the panel approved the plan—with conditions. Mark felt a mix of relief and anxiety. The hardest part was still ahead.

***

Emily studied the newest survey data and walked into Mark's office. "We found a pristine site. Perfect sand."

Mark looked up. "And?"

"An untouched seabed off Wollongong. It's deeper, but perfect sand quality."

"And?"

"And we're not touching it," she said firmly.

A smile crossed Mark's face. "Great work, Emily. Let's prepare the team for a visit."

As they surveyed the Wollongong site, Mark saw the ecosystem through Emily's eyes—teeming with life, a reminder of what they were fighting for. They decided against mining the site, prioritizing conservation over profit. Mark was hopeful they'd find a middle ground.

With a deep breath, he collected the phone and dialed the number for the Environmental Protection Agency. His proposal aimed to ensure the prosperity of both the city and the sea. It was a gamble, but it was one he felt compelled to take.

The conversation was tense, but Mark was persuasive. He outlined a plan for sustainable extraction, one that minimizes damage to the surrounding ecosystem and includes a comprehensive restoration program.

It was a risk, but it was a risk worth taking. The line went silent for a moment before the voice on the other end spoke. "Alright, Mark. Let's do this."

The team sprang into action. They designed a new dredging technique that avoids disturbing the coral and seagrass, using the latest in sonar technology to navigate the underwater maze.

The dredging process gradually unveiled the ocean floor, inch by inch. The sand lived up to their expectations of fineness and abundance, but the marine life was just as impressive.

They worked in harmony, extracting only what they needed while preserving the delicate balance of nature. They danced with precision and respect, a performance never attempted on this scale before.

The days turned into weeks, and the S.S. Meridian grew heavier with each trip. The ship's crew watched the submersibles come and go with a newfound appreciation for the world beneath them. They had become guardians of the hidden realm, and they took their role seriously.

On the last day of the operation, Mark stood on the deck, the wind whipping his hair. The horizon was a blur of blue and gold, a perfect reflection of the challenges they had faced. As the last load arrived, so did the hope for a sustainable future.

As the ship pulled away from the site, Mark felt a sense of accomplishment. They had done it. They had found the sand without causing irreparable harm. But as the coast of Sydney grew smaller in the distance, he knew that this was the beginning.

The real challenge was to come, ensuring their hard-won balance will withstand the increasing pressure of demand. The phone in his pocket buzzed, bringing him back to reality. It was a message from his wife, reminding him of their son's soccer game.

He smiled, knowing that the sand they had delivered will soon be part of the very fabric of the city his family called home.

With a final look at the now-distant dunes of Bondi Beach, Mark turned to his team. "Let's get back to shore," he said. "We've got a city to build, and an ocean to protect."

During the journey back to Sydney, the team reviewed the data from the survey, discussing the potential long-term effects of their work.

They had extracted the sand without damaging the coral reefs, but the seagrass beds will take time to recover. Mark knew that their success was only the first step on a much longer journey.

Government officials, construction magnates, and environmentalists clamored to hear their report. Mark stepped off the ship, feeling the gravity of the situation. The future of marine sand mining in Australia hung in the balance.

He approached the podium with a steady hand; the wind carrying his words to the gathered crowd. "We've provided the materials needed for growth without compromising our marine life," he announced. "This demands that each of us stay watchful and committed."

The response was a mix of applause and skepticism. Environmentalists gave their approval with a nod, while government officials and business moguls exchanged knowing glances. They had made the deal, but the truest test comes in the months and years ahead.

The S.S. Meridian unloaded its cargo with the efficiency of a well-oiled machine. Workers transferred the sand to waiting trucks, destined for the ever-expanding Saudi Arabian desert.

Mark followed the process, imagining the future homes to be built from the meticulously extracted grains. As the ship disappeared into the bustle of the harbor, Mark felt a twinge of pride. The demand for sand was insatiable, and new challenges will arise with every order.

He walked along the waterfront, the sun setting behind the city skyline. The water shimmered with a newfound significance, a reminder of the responsibility that now rested on his shoulders.

The ocean was a vast and complex organism, and it was up to them to ensure that it remained healthy as they continued to tap into its resources.

With the success of the Newcastle site, Mark and his team had earned a reputation for innovation and care. They will be called upon to consult on future projects, to find that delicate balance between progress and preservation.

With the lights of Sydney sparkling like stars in the twilight, Mark realized the arduous work was only beginning.

Months later, Mark stood on the deck of the S.S. Meridian, watching the horizon. The Newcastle operation had been a cautious success, and their techniques were being adopted worldwide. Emily, now a full team member, worked alongside him, her energy infectious.

A call from Dubai offered funding for a research facility, a chance to expand their mission. Mark decided with the same clarity that had guided him from the start. They'd accept the challenge, but on their terms.

The ocean was not a commodity to be bought and sold, but a living entity to be respected and preserved. Mark leaned against the ship's railing, watching the massive conveyor belt transfer golden sand into the hold. Emily approached, her clipboard tucked under her arm.

"Last shipment this quarter," she said.

Mark nodded. "Singapore again?"

"Yep. Land reclamation project," Emily replied. She tapped her pen against the clipboard. "Forty thousand metric tons. Straight from the coastal quarry near Byron Bay."

The conveyor belt hummed, sand cascading in a steady stream. Dust particles caught the late afternoon sun.

"Ever wonder about all this sand?" Mark asked. "We're literally moving mountains, one grain at a time."

Emily shrugged and thought for a moment.

A seagull landed on a nearby stack of empty containers, watching them with a disinterested eye.

"Ecosystem's gotta' feel it though," Mark muttered. "Can't just keep taking it without consequences."

Emily was quiet for a moment. "Regulations are tight now. Environmental assessments, restoration plans. It's not like the old days. Mark, you never rested on your laurels."

Mark blushed as he smiled at her remark.

The last of the sand settled. Mark straightened up, brushing dust from his shirt.

Gesturing to the S.S. Meridian and the crew, Emily said, "That's all thanks to you!"

"Another day," he said.

"Another shipment," Emily finished.

Firmly committed to upholding their values, Mark, with his team, embarked on a new chapter. The S.S. Meridian sailed under a new flag, one that bore the emblem of a sustainable future.

###

Eco-Drama
*The spark for this story came when I read a bit of trivia that Australia sells sand to other countries for use in building material.

Australian Vernacular Guide for 'The Tree and the Tarn'

AUTHOR'S NOTE: IN THE following story, *The Tree and the Tarn*, I've written the dialogue to reflect the distinct pronunciation and expressions of Australian vernacular.

Certain words are spelled phonetically to capture the unique sound and rhythm of Aussie speech, enhancing authenticity while keeping readability in mind.

Narration spelling is in American English.

Synopsis:

In the ancient woods of Tasmania, William Thompson grows up in a close-knit, self-sufficient family that relies on the land for survival.

When William reaches adulthood, his father introduces him to the Thompson family rite of passage, one that will test William's bond to his roots and his readiness to build a future.

Through tradition, resilience, and the artistry of family craftsmanship, William learns what it truly means to carry on his heritage.

For–faw *You*–yah *Nature*–naychuh
Water–wottah *Your*–yoah *Tincture*–teencchuh
Matter–mattah *You're*–yaw *Clear*–cleah
Years–yeahs *Their*–thaeh *Here*–heah
Alright–oolroigh' *They're*–thyah *Cider*–cida
Pour–poah *There*–theah *You've*–yah've
Father–fahthah *Mother*–muhthah *Master*–mahstah
Sweetheart–swaythot "G" is dropped at end of words

Meaning of Odd Words
Brekki–Breakfast **Ciggie**–cigar **Tarn**–lake
Wayalinah–fermented/alcoholic cider gum tree sap **Nointer**–rascal
Jack Jumper–venomous ant **Bugger**–swear word
First Fleet–convict arrival **Moreish**–want to eat more
Fair dinkum–emphasizes genuineness

Author's Note Folk Lore/Romance

The Tree and the Tarn

PART 1: ROOTS TO BRANCHES

LONG AGO, IN THE forests of Tasmania—where trees held the secrets of men's futures within their roots—lived a sheep farmer named William Thompson.

But perhaps I'm getting ahead of myself—William wasn't born a farmer. His life began in a remote corner of the Central Highlands, deep within Tasmania's ancient woods.

Far from other people, he and his parents relied on the land and nature. Medicinal plants, roots, and even the soil they depended on were abundant.

The forest provided plentiful wild game, fish, and other valuable resources, like trees—as it had been for several generations of Thompsons. To tell you about William, I'll share stories within a story.

***

To celebrate the birth of their boy, William, Papa planted a cider gum tree in a large clearing behind the house. William's education, like theirs, came from the land. Papa patiently taught him all he could about their surroundings.

One day, fifteen-year-old William and Papa gathered leaves and roots for Mama to make medicine. Papa spoke to him about how he and Mama had settled in the forest. "William, did I tell yah about when Mama and I decided to stay on this land?"

"No, Papa."

"It began in a canvas tent, cooking ovah a fire pit that we dug with a shovel." Papa's gaze grew distant, his voice softened as he spoke of those first months on the land.

"When yoah mama and I started out heah, we had little more than the canvas on our backs. The tent barely kept out the rain, and food was neva certain.

"I remember us hoistin' up into the trees what we had to keep the creettahs from takin' it. But, well, the possums still got claeva and found thaeh way up."

Papa chuckled as he mimicked the stealthy crawl of a possum with his hand. "Yoah mama came up with the idea to smeah the tent seams with pitch from the alpine ash trees around heah, just to keep the rain out.

"I'd cut chunks o' bark, and we'd heat it slow-like to draw out the pitch—sticky as anythin' and messy too, but it kept us dry on nights when the rain hit hahd.

"The trenchin' was her idea too, taught me to dig channels around the tent for the wottah to drain off. Hahd work, but it saved us from sleepin' in a puddle more than once."

William nodded, his eyes wide, drawn into his father's story.

"But it was food that worried me most," Papa continued, his face growing serious. "One dry spell, we went days on nearly nothin'. We'd lay traps, go fishin' by hand, but luck was scarce.

"Then Mama remembered the native peppa' bush. 'Poison fish with it,' she said, like it was the most nahturul thing in the wohld. I thought she'd lost her mind!"

Papa laughed, but there was respect in his voice. "She knew her plants. Told me to pound up the layves and berries, toss it into the still wottahs, and wait.

"So we did, and before long, fish started goin' belly up, floatin' to the surface like a gift from the lahnd itself."

"Weren't they poisoned?" William asked, wide-eyed.

"Aye, but not for us," Papa replied, tapping his chest. "See, fish braythe it in through gills, but we don't have those, lucky for us. So, we'd scoop 'em up, gut 'em, and cook 'em proper. Yoah mama's knowledge kept us goin', and it was that same knowledge that taught me to respect the forest."

He paused, a look of pride crossing his face. "And that's how yah learn to live off the lahnd. Each bit o' knowledge yah gain, yah pass on, like we're doin' now. It's in yoah blood, boy, just like the pitch on them tent seams was on our hands. The forest teaches yah, but it don't come easy."

Their banter lightened as they worked, gathering roots and herbs for hours more.

Back at the house, William and Papa unloaded their nature haul onto the porch to let Mama pick through and sort to dry.

"William, sweetie, take these layves out back and spread them on the big screen. Don't let any of them touch each uhthah. Bring the dry layves from the uhthah screen. When yah do that, I'll let yah bash some things."

"Yes, Mum."

Mama sorted everything into different piles to plan how best to use them. "Papa, I'm low on stomach teencchuh so tomorra bring back a basket of peppa' layves and, eh, three juicy peppa' tree twigs." She set the rolling pin and mortar and pestle out for William so he could help make the pastes and ointments.

"Aye. And the spirits?" Papa asked.

"Afta this batch, I need two jugs of vodka and, eh, two bottles of glycerin."

William returned with a basket of dried leaves. "Heah yah go. Can I bash now?"

"Start by usin' the roller to flatten the rhizomes and roots in that pile. Mash. Don't beat or bash."

As a local healer, Mama made tinctures, salves, teas, and ointments to treat the country folk. These items traded for higher quantities of flour than anything else Mama created.

"Mama, how'd yah learn so much about this medicine makin'?"

"I was born knowin' I reckon. Every day, Mama and Granny took me into the woods, just like Papa does with yah. It's tradition. Important things must be passed down, lest we forget."

"Papa taught me how to catch fish and birds using herbs."

"Aye, and it'll serve yah well to remembah and pass it on to yoah kids. Like Papa teachin' yah to wheettle and carve. Look how good yah are."

William contributed to the household by working with wood and whittling doll-like figures from tree limbs. He traded small carved toys with nearby people during Christmas.

Wooden dowels and pins don't rust, so farmers bought the ones he carved from willow branches. They were useful for holding straps, tools, and other hangy-dangly things. During hard times, he traded for flour and animal fat.

Papa didn't abide mischievous behavior, but sometimes Mama hid a grin when William's antics got the better of her.

Now, at seventeen, William was developing difficult emotions and feelings. To unleash frustration and anxiety, he climbed his favorite tree.

William climbed higher than ever, feeling invincible—right up until his grip slipped—hitting the ground with a thud, the breath knocked clean out of him.

"Time to eat!" Mama called.

When William didn't respond, Papa went looking and found him at the tree. "Oi, are yah livin'?"

Gasp. "Aye." *Gasp.* "I took a bit of a tumble, theah, I reckon."

***

"Aye, yah did that for a fact." Papa's voice softened, his gaze drifting up to the tree's canopy.

William lay on his back, gazing at the rustling leaves above. The sweet fragrance of the leaves reminded him of his childhood and the eucalyptus bouquets he'd bring to Mama, always making her smile. It made him happy every time.

The two sat quietly, lost in their memories, until Papa reached out a hand to help him up.

Back in the house, everyone has gone to bed. Sitting slumped at the bed's edge, Papa seemed to carry the weight of the world. "It's time, Mama. It's time to have the talk with William. I've dreaded it. We haven't had enough time with him."

"I know, Papa. But it's tradition. We've raised him up the best we could. He's a fine young man—honest, hardworking, and funny. It's all yah can want in a fella."

"Aye, I saw him today, layin' at the bottom of the cida gum tree, strugglin' with all the questions about where his life might lead. Get some sleep. I'll talk to him, tomorra."

"Aye. I love yah, Papa."

"Aye. I love yah, Mama."

Part II: The Rite of Passage

Mama was up before dawn, bustling in the kitchen before William and Papa started stirring. She moved about lighting the oil lamps and building a fire in the stove.

Soon, the crackling wood filled the kitchen with its comforting warmth. Her hands—buried in a flour mixture—she folded and shaped the dough into a rustic loaf.

While the bread was baking, Mama set a pot of water to boil. This morning, William's efforts preparing roots for storage paid off. She took a jar of chicory powder from the shelf—the chicory roots that William and Papa had gathered, cut, roasted, and ground, ready to be brewed.

The smell of fresh bread soon wafted through the house, more effective than a crowing cock. The chicory coffee added its nutty, woody aroma to the already fragrant kitchen.

"Mmm, mornin', Mama. Yah smell delicious," Papa teased as he entered.

"Mornin', Papa—yah look delicious," she replied, letting a girlish giggle escape.

"Oi! Yah feelin' a tad impish this morn', are yah?"

"Sit. I'll poah the coffee."

She sliced the loaf and plated it with bowls of rolled oats, nuts, and berries. William joined them, bright-eyed and cheery.

"Mornin', sweetie," Mama greeted, handing Papa a cup and then turning to extinguish the lamps as the sun began to light the kitchen.

Papa cleared his throat. "We need to take a walk today, William. Not to gatha' anythin', but to talk about business."

"What kind of business?"

"Man business. So, eat yah fill; it may be a long walk."

"Aye."

***

After breakfast, they prepared for the walk. William thought he should feel nervous, but he had a peculiar calmness about him.

"Papa, did yah and Pops have a walk?"

"Aye, I was about the age yah are." Papa reached for his pocket knife and clipped a small twig, whittling on it as they walked. "Pops said, 'Today is special for yah, and I want to give yah somethin' to remember it by.' Then he handed me his pocket knife."

"Aye, she's a beaut."

"And now, this knife is yours."

"Papa, I can't take that knife."

"See this handle?" He held up the honey-brown handle, its gnarled bird's-eye grain buffed smooth from years of use. "Pops carved this from the small limb of a Huon Pine when he reached the age yah are." Papa put a firm hand on William's shoulder but remained silent.

"Are these some family traditions Mama talks about? One day, I reckon I'll be handin' this knife off to my son."

"Aye, son, traditions, beliefs, and rites of passage made the Thompson name what it is today."

"Rite of passage? Reckon I'm not too cleah on what that means, Papa."

"Yah know about Aboriginal walkabout? In the yeahs before a young man's walkabout, he's prepared by the eldas—given advice on survivin' and approachin' adulthood.

"They get knowledge about the land, home, and ancestors from thaeh tribes. They've done it ova many generations."

"Mama passed on medicine makin' to me, and you passed on how to catch food. So I won't starve, I reckon?"

"Aye, this is true. Yah've learned a lot."

"Tell me about the Thompson family rite of passage, Papa."

"Oi. The Thompson lineage dates back over a century. The maytriachs are the healers and naytuhalists. The paytriachs are the hunters and gatherers, bringing in what nature has to offer.

"Today, we aren't huntahs or gathurahs—we are here for yer rite of passage, the same one my forefathers completed at your age.

"To outsidahs, it may seem strange, but to the male family membahs, it's tradition."

Papa's voice softened, but there was a noticeable heaviness to his tone. "William, it's time for yah to marry."

William froze. "I don't know many girls. Where would I look?"

"Aye, that's where the tradition part comes in. Yaw goin' to cut the cida gum tree down."

"I can't cut the cida gum! It's been me friend–me comfort. When it weeps, I treat myself to its toffee apple sap. I let it run into the trunk where it ferments into wayalinah, and I drink my fill."

"Aye, that stuff is moreish. But this is how it must be."

"Why? How does fellin' the tree teach me anythin', much less get a wife?"

"Oi! Yah need to trust what I'm tellin' yah. After yah cut the tree, I'll explain the tale that started it all."

Papa's firm tone filled William with trust, though inside he balked at the idea of cutting down his favorite tree.

Mama, waiting on the porch with tea and lunch, noticed William's slouched shoulders and knew that Papa had instructed him to cut the tree. "Oi! Fellas, come eat. It's been a long day for yah both."

"Mama, I'm not hungry. I'll take a drink with me to the cida tree." She passed him the glass silently, her expression unreadable.

William walked slowly, as if his feet were mired in mud. At the tool shed, he paused, and the hinges let out a lonesome creak as he opened the door. Setting his glass down, he reached for a heavy canvas rucksack.

Pops' Hults Bruk felling axe hung from willow pegs on the wall. The brutal, razor-sharp blade beckoned him from its hickory handle. Reaching beside the ax, he added a wedge and a sledge hammer to the rucksack. Then, he lifted the ax itself.

Hefting the rucksack over his shoulder, William picked up his glass and made his way to the cider gum tree. He placed the tools on the ground near the tree base.

His mind felt overwhelmed, trying to process what was to come. He broke off a twig and took in its familiar smell. Sipping his tea, he sat against the tree and leaned back.

How many times did Mama put yoah layves into hot wottah so I could inhale the vapours and open me sinuses? He remembered the time she'd used oil and sap from the tree to stop that fierce itch from jack jumper bites.

I'll salvage as much of yah as I can. I'll craft planks for a table, for me wife and me to gatha around. The rest will make a marital bed for me family.

He sighed, letting his gaze wander up into the canopy. *This tree's seen me childhood, me dreams. Am I ready to sever that bond, leaving the familiar behind for an unknown future? If I have to cut my tree, then so be it.*

William stood, looking at the rucksack.

The hickory handle peeked out at him.

He hesitated. This tree was his comfort.

He gripped the linseed-oiled handle, swinging the ax half-heartedly. Three times, he struck. With each thwack, he winced, feeling as though he were hitting himself. A sudden gust nudged him closer to the tree, its leaves whispering in the wind.

Finally, after pouring his spirit, tears, and sweat into felling the tree, it began to creak and pop. He looked up at the leaf canopy, feeling a calm akin to standing in a cathedral.

He raised the sledge and wedge, driving them in.

The rustling foliage sang like a soft hymn.

Wood chips flew as he swung harder, more deliberately. The thud of ax strikes echoed through the forest.

Bark in hues of cream, pale pink, and brown fell around him like tears.

A bullet-like crack rang out as larger limbs broke under the force of the fall. *As simple as that,* he thought. *My future depends on a felled tree.*

The cider gum tree landed, pointing south.

William turned back, the rucksack full of tools over his shoulder, and saw Mama resting her head on Papa's chest as they waited on the porch.

"I'll clean the tools and sharpen the axe and be at the house in a bit," William said humbly.

Later, they sat quietly on the porch, letting the cool evening breeze wash over them. "The first cut yah make in the tree determines the direction the tree falls," Papa said.

"Aye. I didn't plan where she'd land. I let her decide for herself, I reckon."

"That's the way it's meant to be. I couldn't tell yah anythin' about the tradition. Yah could neva have outside influences. Pops neva said why I had to cut my tree until it was done."

"Yoah tree? What was yoah's?"

"It was a swamp gum. A bugger to fell because she grew so tall. It's been a day for yah. Go wash up and rest."

"Aye. G'night, Mama. Papa."

"I'll tell yah more about the rite tomorra. G'night."

The next morning, William sipped his tea, mulling over why he had to cut his favorite tree.

Papa leaned back and said, "Oi! I'll help yah make the planks from yoah tree if yah like. I've got experience makin' furniture. The table yaw eatin' off is from my tree."

Imagining the pieces they could create, William murmured, "Maybe we can carve a headboard... add cida gum layves etched along the edges."

Mama, pulling a basket of fresh berries from the cupboard, chimed in, "If yah still have some agriculchuh vinega and wire sponge left, I'll make a stain for the table from the black raspberries yah gatha'd. They'll give it a rich, dark finish." With plans made, they began their work that afternoon.

For days, Papa and William stripped bark—turning logs into sturdy planks—dust swirling in beams of light. Papa's knife made quick work of the rough edges, and soon, the sharp scent of freshly cut wood filled the air. William, still new to the craft, focused intently, guiding the blade along the grain.

Mama set up a makeshift workshop on the porch, arranging baskets of fresh and dried berries around her. She hummed softly, her fingers darkened by the berries' juices as she mixed them into the vinegar for her stain.

Smiling, she brushed the table's rough surface with the mixture, adding layers of color and life. "It'll be good and ready for yah someday," she'd say, winking at William.

As they shaped the dining table, William watched his father's hands move with practiced precision. "Oi, yah make it look easy," he muttered, brushing shavings from his arms.

Papa chuckled, eyes bright with pride. "Yah'll be doin' this in yoah sleep soon enough. Besides, a family table holds more than meals, son—it holds the stories of those who sit around it."

In the evenings, they worked by lantern light, each lost in thought. William carved intricate leaves along the edges of the headboard, letting his hands follow the memory of the canopy that had once shaded him.

As he smoothed the last burrs and knots, he couldn't help but feel the spirit of the tree filling the room with warmth.

Over several weeks, the family worked together, each pouring a part of themselves into the pieces that would soon furnish William's new home.

By the time they had finished, the dining table, headboard, and crib seemed almost alive, brimming with the love and history they'd woven into every piece.

Part III: Take Heed the Way the Tree Falls

William whittled as Papa carved details into a piece of wood. "Papa, how long have the men in our family been felling a tree?"

"Aye, been a while."

"Why do we do it?"

"Oi! I'll tell yah the story as it was told to me. In the late 1890s, a Roma caravan passed through on the way to Hobart.

"This was some yeahs after the gipsies arrived in Austruylia as convicts on the First Fleet. Their wagon broke down, and there was no sign of homes or people in sight. Vadoma, a soothsaya, told Janos, the leada, 'Go alone into the forest and cut down a random tree. Take heed of the way the tree falls. Walk in the direction the tree pointed, and yah will find help.'

"Janos walked in the direction the tree fell, trudgin' through the dense forest. He noticed that some trees were dead or dyin' among the livin'.

"Later, he told stories to the caravan kids, watchin' thaeh eyes sparkle as he described the dyin' trees, which looked to him like the bleached skeletons of beached whales. Even in death, naychuh was real beauty to him.

"Janos saw a cleahin' and came upon a cabin, somethin' from another time, sittin' on thirty logs of Huon Pine timba."

William perked up. "Oi! That's the same wood Pops used for his knife handle!"

Papa nodded and continued. "The people knew the 2,000-year-old Huon trees—some are even older—thy're impu'vious to rot. Yah can use dead logs that've been lyin' around for centuries. But back to my story.

"Shiny spots peeked through the rust on the tin roof, and the weather and neglect had made the porch unsafe to walk on. The chimney, patched with rusty tin sheetin', had a trail of smoke risin' from it—a welcome sight for Janos.

"He knocked, callin' out, 'I'm Janos. I mean no harm, but I need help for my people.'

"A middle-aged couple answered. 'Hello, I'm Cha'lie Thompson, and this is my wife, Sophie. Yah must be hungry, yayh?'

"Janos replied, 'I could eat a horse and chase down the rider for dessert!' They invited him in with a grin. 'Come inside for tucker. We've got some dampa, smoked fish, and biscuits.'

"Janos stepped carefully onto the porch, deemin' it safe, and walked into the house. 'Dampa?' he asked.

"'D a m p e r, is bread,' Cha'lie said with a chuckle. 'Takes the edge off yoah hunga'. Sophie knows her biscuits too. We trade for the best butter in the land so she can treat us to sweet bikkies.'

"Janos thanked Cha'lie, explainin' that his caravan had to stop at the forest edge when a vardo wheel spindle broke. He asked if Cha'lie had tools he could borrow.

"Cha'lie reassured him, 'No worries; I work with wood all the time. I'll gatha' some spindles, chisels, and hammahs. Yah sit and eat.'

"He muttered somethin' to Sophie, who nodded and took up two flour sacks. While Cha'lie gathered tools in his shed, Sophie packed the sacks with as much food as they could spare.

"Cha'lie loaded the tools in his cart, and they returned with Janos to the caravan, where everyone worked togethah to repair the wheel.

"Aftah they'd eaten, the caravan folks invited the couple to stay and fellowship. Vadoma led the women in dancin' around the fire, their skirts whirl'n like dervishes.

"As the music slowed and the dancers stepped back from the fire, Vadoma took a limb from the tree Janos had cut. When it glowed red in the fire, she pulled it from the flames and tamped it into the dirt, drawin' a crude etchin' as she spoke.

"She said, 'A dog that travels finds bones. Only love lightens any burden. Be wise: Walk in the path of love.' Handin' the stick to Cha'lie and Sophie, she said, 'Each time yah and yoah heirs give birth to a boy, plant a tree to honor the friendships made here today.

"'Each boy should have a different type of tree. Tell him nothin' of this day. He grows with the tree, untouched by outside influences.

"'The tree absorbs his aura and rewards him if he's pure of heart. When he reaches manhood, have him cut the tree and heed the way it falls.

"'Tell him why he cut it, and he's to walk in that direction. If he walks far, he will find a wife—an honorable one.'

"Cha'lie and Sophie were my grandparents. We've kept this tradition and rite of passage for every boy born since. William, you'll plant a different tree for each son yah have, and they'll each fell and follow thaeh tree."

"Oi! How can yah keep somethin' like that a secret?" William asked.

"Aye, we do it, and will keep doin' it until it stops workin'."

William remembered a girl—a perfect girl—he'd met on a nearby sheep farm to the south. *That suits me!*

"Papa, what direction did yah go to find Mama?"

Part IV: Reflections at the Tarn

Over time, William's slender frame transformed, his muscles defined but natural, shaped more by work than by vanity. His build was strong but lean, a testament to the steady, grounding rhythm of life in the Highlands.

With no facial hair to hide it, his prominent jawline and natural pout were always visible. Years of hauling heavy logs had molded him into a strong young man.

Mama and Papa helped William make furniture from the cider gum tree, knowing the time was near for him to walk away.

William groomed himself, donned his Sunday suit, and polished his shoes for the journey. Mama came out of the cabin holding a small flour sack with biscuits and smoked fish. "Yah stay safe out there, and keep a smile on yoah face, William."

"No worries, Mama."

"Wait here. I have somethin' for yah to give to the lady yah choose." Mama returned carrying a bouquet of dried flowers, leaves, and bark from the cider gum tree.

"Mama, I can't give away yoah bouquet. I made that for yah."

"Aye, and I give it back so yah can make another lady smile." Mama hugged him tight, kissed his cheek, and stepped back inside the cabin. William fetched his walking staff and filled his water canteen.

Papa shook William's hand, saying, "I know yah will choose well," then went inside to be with Mama.

William's goal today was to reach the tarn at the edge of vast farmlands. He had walked for several hours, taking rest stops before seeing the mountain lake.

Although surrounded by gentle rolling hills, he knew people lived beyond the tarn. His heart was set on seeing one special person.

At the tarn, William treated himself to a nip of smoked fish and a refreshing dip. The amphitheater-like valley, formed by a glacier, was a source of happiness for him—much like the cider gum tree.

He found a shaded spot and unburdened himself of his flour sack, bouquet, staff, and clothing. Alone, he savored the solitude, feeling utterly free in the secluded tarn. His arms stretched toward the sky as he breathed in the pine-scented air.

Ruffling his brown hair, he prepared for the cold water, stepping closer to the edge. The crystal-clear, turquoise water revealed pebbles scattered along the lakebed.

Schools of tiny fish shimmered below the surface—a fluid silver mass scuttled away as he stepped in—the icy tinge on his skin stealing his breath. He inhaled deeply and let his body collapse into the cool water.

William let nature take over as he floated, drifting across the lake until only his face remained above water.

After cutting down his cider gum tree, which had pointed south, he knew it was a sign—to find a partner and make a family. Her name was Willow Clarke, the daughter of a sheep farmer. Being here, on the Clarke family farm, was the closest he'd been to farm life.

Drifting into a near sleep, his thoughts turned to Willow. Shy by nature, he'd felt at ease talking to her. During a scallop harvesting trip to Hobart, he'd seen her sitting on a boulder, nuzzling a sheep.

Her smile could light the night.

She usually wore her hair in a bun, but one day a breeze had tossed it free—a deep mahogany with subtle amber highlights.

I bet she smells like leatherwood flowers.

A sudden splash nearby snapped him from his thoughts. He cocked one eye toward the shore and made out the shadowed outline of a person. Another splash followed as they tossed a pebble at him.

He was shocked to see anyone here—especially with himself fully exposed. Rolling over, he bobbed in the water, facing the shoreline. The person waved. He knew right away who it was.

"William!"

"Oi! No way! Willow?"

"Aye. Did I catch yah at a bad time?"

"I'd say awkward."

"Well, don't let me keep yah from comin' ashore," she said, forming a sly smile.

"Could I bother yah to bring somethin' to cover myself?"

"Sure." Willow sauntered to the shade, where his clothes lay across a small boulder. She glanced over her options, selecting something suitable and hiding it behind her back as she stepped closer to the water.

"Put it down and turn around," William said.

"As yah wish." Stifling a giggle, she placed the bouquet on the ground and turned away.

"Oi! Not funny." William held the bouquet over his important parts.

Willow's laughter, bright as morning, faded to a pensive smile as she took in his form. She gawked as he walked to get his pants.

In a quick motion, she hid her face behind her hands, peeking through her fingers. His build was powerful but unassuming, each muscle a testament to his life outdoors, not to any effort to impress.

His skin is rich, almond-colored, smooth and unblemished. I neva seen anythin' like him befowah.

Glancing back at her, he said, "Yoah not peekin', are yah?"

Her cheeks turned rosy pink. "Neva! I'm a lady."

"Aye. That yah are." His face softened as he looked at her. "Whadyah doin' out so far from the farm?"

"I had to wrangle up a wayward dam and her baby. I came here to relax. Why are yah here?"

"Come have a seat. Honest? I'm on my way to see yah."

"Is it scallop harvest time?"

"No. My only agenda is to see yah."

Her face scrunched in delight and confusion. *Her nose is so small and cute. Reminds me of a delicate seashell,* he thought. She sat on the ground, leaning back against the boulder. Brushing water droplets from his hands, he extended the bouquet to her.

"This is for yah. It's made of bits and pieces from my tree."

"Yoah tree? Wait! Yah mean *yoah* tree, don't yah?"

"Yah know about the tree tradition?"

"I know too well. At birth, I had a twin brother. Father planted a willow tree for Noah, and they decided to name me Willow, just like the tree.

"Noah didn't survive past his first birthday. Fahthah was deeply affected by it." William place his hand on her shoulder and pulled it back after a pause. Willow smiled, knowing William felt sad for her.

"Fahthah was familiar with the tradition followed by the people in the Central Highlands. That practice led to many large happy families. He wanted nothin' but happiness for Noah. What was yoah tree, William?"

Unfurling the flour sack with the smoked fish and biscuits, William said, "I'm sorry about Noah. A cida gum. My tree was a cida gum." He sat next to Willow and offered her food, which she accepted with a smile.

"Oi! This fish is moreish. Where'd yah buy it?"

"Papa and I smoke them ourselves to sell. We trade it when times are bad."

Willow and William leaned against a shaded boulder, their conversation light but warm as they shared stories and laughter.

"Tell me about yoah family. I often think of yah after seein' yah durin' yoah scallop harvest trips," Willow said.

"Our family has lived in remote areas of the Central Highlands for generations. Mama and Papa's livelihood comes from various means.

"Since fishin' comes easy for me and Papa, we smoke enough to sell so people can rely on it durin' winta."

"If this is what yah smoke, I'd love to buy some next time yah pass through."

"I couldn't take money from yah."

"Yah said earlier yah trade when times are hard. Would yah trade for lamb meat, or some wool for yoah Mama? We have the best Herdwick sheep in the land."

"Aye, that sounds great. We come from a long line of traders. There are things we don't grow that others do, and that's as good as money.

"When I was actin' up, Papa would send me into the forest to gatha unique wood. He knew it'd calm me down. When I found gnarled limbs, I'd turn them into art and sell or trade them for food.

"Papa let me use Pops' knife to wheettle small figures and dolls. As Christmas approached, those gained popularity for tradin'."

"William, I'd love to see one of ya' dolls."

"Aye, maybe one will find its way in yer Christmas stocking."

"What about yer mum? Does she work?"

"Mama doesn't have steady work, but when she does midwife duties, she's paid in flour and herbs. Her biggest contribution is makin' scallop pies to sell to locals.

"That's why I make scallop trips to the midlands. That was me first glimpse of yah."

William shifted, moving a little closer to Willow as he sat down. "I stopped here at this spot for a nip and a dip. After leavin' here, I kept walkin' south, and I saw yah tendin' the sheep on yoah family farm.

"Yah and that dog workin' the herd—that intense look on yoah face did somethin' to me. I was smitten."

"Oh, I reckon I'm blushin'. My ears are hot." Willow fanned her face and giggled.

"Sorry, didn't mean to embarrass yah. I often think of yah and miss yah when yah leave."

"Aye, I feel the same way. I've met several young men, but I have no feelins for them."

"Oi! How many of them have yah seen naked?"

"Good point. Yoah the only one. Worth the wait, that's for true."

"Now I reckon I'm blushin'."

"Are yah still comin' to see me? We can pretend this meetin' didn't happen. Yah can meet my mum and dad."

"Aye, I will. Yah think yoah dad will take kindly to a bogan like me?"

"I'm of the mind Dad wasn't fond of schoolin' in his youth either. Yah'll fit in just fine. Mum will love yah." Willow stood and brushed the dust off her skirt. "OK, I'll see yah 'round dinnah time, I imagine?"

"Count on it."

For a moment, time paused, letting friendship bloom in the tranquil embrace of nature.

Part V: The Lamb and the Tobacco Leaf

William stood tall, putting on his best smile as he extended a fist to knock on Willow's door. Her mum opened the door, her expression radiating sunshine.

William's eyes darted over her shoulder, searching for her dad. Before he could say much, her mum pulled him in, kissing him on each cheek. He felt a bit uncertain about the interaction. *Maybe hugs and kisses are a proper greetin' when enterin' the house.*

"Mum, I want yah to meet William Thompson," Willow said, accepting the bouquet he offered.

"William, meet my mum, Ava Clarke."

"Pleasure to meet yah, ma'am," he said, bringing her hand to his lips to kiss her knuckles.

The aroma of roasted lamb and vegetables filled the air, easing any tension. Willow took his hand and led him into the house.

"Willow, swaythot, get him a drink while I finish the vegetables, yeah? Yoah dad will be down in a minute."

"Beer or wine?" Willow asked.

"Soda or tea is fine." A knot formed in William's stomach as he heard her dad's footfalls on the staircase. Willow placed a reassuring hand on her dad's elbow, guiding him toward William.

"Dad, meet William Thompson."

"William, my dad, George Clarke." The two men extended their hands and shook firmly, each exuding quiet confidence.

"Clarke? Sir, are yah the Clarke tobacco namesake?"

"Aye, but only distantly. I'm the black sheep—I wanted somethin' different for my family. With hard work, we've turned this bare 1,000 acres into what yah see today."

"Aye, wonderful job, indeed."

"Yoah in for a treat tonight. Ava's a wonderful cook. Plus, she's teachin' Willow a few things." George gestured for everyone to join Ava at the dining table. She stood at one end, waiting as George claimed his seat at the other. William and Willow sat facing each other.

George gave a blessing. "Everyone, join hands, please. As we gather around this table to share this meal, we are mindful of Your abundant blessings. Bless this food we are about to receive. May it nourish our bodies and sustain us through a time of fellowship today. Amen."

Everyone nodded their heads, murmuring, "Amen." George served William first. "Our lamb is tender milk-fed, and it's a decadent experience. No chewy bits here. We promise." He spooned a hearty serving of lamb and vegetables onto William's plate.

Ava drizzled a golden liquid over William's vegetables. "Muttonbird oil is exceptional and will make a vahst improvement in the taste of yoah food."

"Oi! If it's that good, yah might have to roll me out of here!" he teased.

Ava chuckled. "Please, eat yoah fill. I made apple sponge cake with leatherwood honey as a topper."

I bet Willow smells like leatherwood blossoms. "Yah have honeycombs yoahself, do yah, Mr. Clarke?"

"Aye, we do. Call me George. When trees flower in Decembah, we'll relocate hives to the leatherwood tree area. Yah wake up in the mornin', and smell that smell—it's hard to describe it. The bees start workin' to harvest the nectar. The flowerin' trees are so profuse that from a piece away, the area looks covered with snow."

"I'd like to smell that." William caught himself looking straight at Willow when he said that. "I mean, I'd like to see that." His ears burned, and Willow's cheeks blushed slightly.

"Don't be a stranga and come around more," George said, pushing himself away from the table and patting his overfilled belly.

"Holy dooley! Ma'am, sir, this was a real fair dinkum spread. Can't recall eatin' this fine, eva."

"Fancy a ciggie, William? Made with top-notch Clarke tobacco." Admiring its quality, George rolled the cigar between his thumb and forefinger. He lifted it to his lip, taking a long inhale, savoring the scent. Honey and caramel notes from the wrapper mingled with the rich aroma of coffee-scented tobacco.

"I've neva smoked. Wouldn't know how."

Slipping a second cigar into his vest pocket, George put an arm over William's shoulder. "Let's go outside for a bit." On the porch, George held out his cigar, explaining how to cut the tip and light it.

"Tapered at the head, a torpedo-shaped ciggie gives a nice concentration of flayvah. Whatevah size or shape yah prefa, it's best to be conservative with yoah first cut." George slipped the head into a guillotine cutter. Squeezing the blades together, he let the small cap piece fall to the floor. With a swish of his foot, George kicked it into the dirt.

"Test the draw with the ciggie in yoah mouth, and cut a little more if yah need. Lightin' takes patience to get a good, even burn.

"Remembah toastin' the perfect golden-brown marshmallow? You don't put it in the flame but hold it above, cookin' it slow and even. Same goes for lightin' a fine ciggie. Keep it above the flame, rotatin' it gradually until the whole end is burnin'.

"When the tobacco starts glowin', draw once or twice to check if it's even. If not, keep rollin' the ciggie above the flame 'til yah get a nice, consistent ash."

George's eyes remained closed, his voice reverent. "Takes time to mahstah, but don't rush it."

William's face showed equal parts curiosity and awkwardness. This ritual looked like a sacred experience. George opened his eyes, casting a sideways look at him. "Yah know, if I were a scoundrel, I'd watch yah smoke it alone. Watch yah get sick and turn green.

"Right before yah're about to vomit, yoah cheeks go pale, lips turn white, and yoah eyes half-close. I'd laugh—that's what my fahthah did to me." George shivered at the memory. "But I wouldn't wish that on anyone. So here's a few secrets.

"Ciggies are for tastin', not inhalin'. Yah draw the smoke into yoah mouth, savor it, then exhale. The rest comes with experience: choosin' the right one, cuttin' and lightin' it, puffin' at the right pace.

"Then there's storin' them right, not over-ashin', and pairin' with whiskey, rum, or coffee. Yah'll learn to enjoy the whole experience. And I hope I haven't lost yah on my meanin' here.

"Yah put a fine woman in place of a fine ciggie, and masterin' the nuances brings just as much pleasure."

"Yes, sir. Hope yah won't be offended if I wait 'til next time for a slow smoke?"

"I'd enjoy that very much, young man. Are yah goin' back home tonight? That's a mighty walk."

"I'll walk back to the tarn and rest until dawn, then strike out again."

"Yah need a horse or buggy. Never know when yah might come across a young lady needin' a ride."

"Papa is usin' the team to pull a few logs from the forest. I'll have a mount next time we meet."

"Aye, good man. Why don't yah stay in the barn, yonda? Ava's savoury toast is excellent. About daybreak, we'll have a cock-a-doodle-doo dish togetha, then yah can be on yoah way."

"I have no doubts about her cookin'. There yah found yoahself a fine lady, Mr. Clarke."

"Thank yah. I'm certain yah've found a fine lady, too. G'night, William. Get rested."

"Seeyah, mate."

William bedded down in the hay overlooking the lambing pens. Sleep came fast and soundly.

In the night, an odd noise woke William. Unfamiliar with the area, he found any commotion strange. Unknown to him, the herding dog was also in the barn, and it had gone out to relieve itself.

William softly spoke to the dog, hoping to keep it calm and avoid any surprises. Curling up a short distance away, the dog lay back down, ignoring him for the rest of the night.

At dawn, one rooster's crow woke William, who had slept lightly with the dog beside him. The proud rooster pranced around him, crowing in circles. Willow was an hour into her chores when William emerged from the barn.

Perfect timing brought Ava's call from the house. She stood with a metal triangle in hand, beaming with that look of sunshine. "Brekkie is ready! Come get it while it's hot!" A pro at the food triangle, her clangs could be heard for miles.

William hung back a bit, waiting for Willow to get closer to the barn. "Mind if I walk yah in?" Her answer was in her wide, bright smile.

"Mornin', sunshine. Yah ready for a new day?"

"Aye. Yah been busy?"

"Days start early heah."

"What's the dog's name?"

"Kirra. It means 'beautiful woman'."

"Aye, so that's yoah middle name?"

"Ooh, smooth one there. My middle name is Grace."

"Pretty. Fits yah," William said, pushing a strand of hair off her face.

The clangs of the triangle quieted as they stepped onto the porch.

"G'day, Mrs. Clarke."

"Hello, William. Did yah sleep well?"

"Sure did. Kirra and I had a quiet night. I'm grateful for the lodgin'."

"Aye, Kirra's a swaythot. She'll love yah foreva now, like family. Come wash up and eat. George left earlia, but he told me to wish yah safe travels until next time." She handed him a case with four hand-rolled Clarke cigars.

"I'll be sure to thank him soon. Gosh, yah have great smells comin' from the kitchen again. George said yah make a fine savoury toast. I've neva had it, and I'm excited to try somethin' new."

Ava blushed. "Savoury toast was a staple at picnics and Grandmuthah's afternoon teas. I kept a pot of hot soup on the stove and savoury toast for Willow after school, especially in winta. I'll pass the recipe to her when she's ready to start her family."

Topped with cheese, eggs, and tomato relish, the toast was pure comfort food. William cut into it, stretching melted cheese across the plate and dripping a bit onto his chin.

They ate in silence, but Willow and Ava exchanged glances, enjoying the pleasure William clearly took in every bite.

"Oi! This is moreish, for sure. Could hold its own against Mama's scallop pie."

"I had scallop pie from a bakery not long ago on a trip to Hobart. Tasty. I've neva tried bakin' scallops myself—fear I'd ruin 'em," Ava said.

"Mama and yah'd get along in the kitchen."

"I'd love to meet yoah parents. Could it be soon?"

"Aye, soon. Now, if yah beg pardon, I've got to get back to help Papa."

Willow slid her chair back and walked William outside. "When yah reckon to be stoppin' back by heah?"

"How about Friday at the tarn around lunch?" William reached for her hand, lifted it to his lips, and kissed her knuckles.

"Sounds fine and dandy." Willow went up on her tiptoes, kissed William on each cheek, and lingered, looking deep into his eyes. *Boomer! I can't wait.*

As he walked away, he glanced over his shoulder to see if she was watching. She was, watching him with a warm smile. Feeling a thrill in his chest, he turned and continued his walk back to the tarn.

Part VI: Where the Home Fires Still Burn

Arriving at the tarn, William sat on a small boulder under the shade of a Huon Pine. *I should reach home a bit befoah dark.* A sadness washed over him as he leaned against the tree to drink from his canteen. *This tree feels nothin' like my cider gum.*

Reflecting on his visit with Willow and her family, he thought, *I can see myself with her for the rest of my life. George and Ava seemed to approve of me. Even Kirra likes me. When a stranger's dog likes yah, that's the seal of approval.*

Gripping his hand-carved staff, he set off for home, the spring in his step returning. Thoughts of Willow danced through his mind, bringing a song to his lips.

> *Cane cutter, cane cutter*
> *Chop, chop, chop! Hear the cane knives ringin'!*
> *Harvestin' the crop; No time for singin'.*
> *Swish, swish, swish,*
> *Hear the cane leaves rustlin';*
> *Only thing we wish is more time for hustlin'.*
> *Load, load, load! Every creaky wagon,*
> *Send 'em on the road with their sides a-saggin'.*

(Lyrics adapted from a traditional Queensland folk song related to cane cutting.)

William reached home before dark, and the chimney smoke let him know dinner would be waiting. Mama greeted him with a hug and sat him at the table.

Between bites, he took deep breaths to keep talking, his excitement barely contained as he told Mama and Papa about his visit with Willow and her parents.

The fervor with which he ate and spoke held his audience captive. Pleased to see him so happy, Mama and Papa held hands and smiled, watching their young man with pride.

William slowed his eating and talking. "Oi! I reckon we can have them all ovah for dinna' soon, yeah?"

Mama appeared startled by the question. "Aye. Did yah tell 'em how we're livin' heah?"

"Whaddayah mean?" William asked.

Papa said, "Well, son, most folks have powa' in thaeh homes now. Yoah muhthah still cooks with a fire she builds, and lights the kitchen with oil lamps."

"Aye, yeah, I nevah minded livin' like we do. Didn't enter my mind sayin' anythin' negative about either of yah."

Mama walked over, running her hand through his hair and pulling his head to her lips. "I do love yah so much. How about we have a picnic lunch at the edge of the forest instead of deennah?"

"Good thinkin', Mama! Wouldn't have thought of that meself."

"When are we to have this meetin'?" Mama asked.

"I need to use the horse and buggy to ride ovah and give Willow a tour of the ranch. I'll get them all agreed to a day then, I reckon."

"Oi! Like Mum and Dad, did yah?" Papa asked.

"They're nice folks. The dog likes me."

"When a stranger's dog likes yah, that's the seal of approval, I reckon," Papa said.

After several weeks today William would finally introduce his best friend, Willow, to Mama and Papa. The plan was simple: a picnic at the edge of the forest.

The sun was out, and a gentle breeze danced through the trees. Mama had prepared all the food, especially her famous fried chicken.

Willow fidgeted with her hair nervously as they arrived at the meeting spot. George and Ava followed closely, their expressions a mix of curiosity and apprehension. Introducing parents could be tricky. William sensed the tension in the air. *What if they didn't get along?*

Mama and Papa were already setting up the blanket. Mama smiled warmly as she saw them approach, her welcoming nature quickly easing the atmosphere.

"Hey, everyone!" she called out, waving as if inviting them into her embrace. Papa offered George a hearty handshake, easing the tension further.

They all sat down, and Ava examined the spread. "This looks delicious. What did yah make?" she asked with genuine interest.

Mama beamed. "Just some fried chicken, my special recipe. It's a family favorite." William felt a sense of pride. Mama's chicken had a way of breaking down walls and bringing people together.

As they ate, the conversation flowed. They talked about life in the Highlands, stories from school, and forest adventures. George shared tales from his own childhood, drawing laughs from everyone.

The atmosphere grew more relaxed, and William felt himself unwinding. The distant chirping of birds and rustling leaves added to the peaceful setting.

But then the conversation hit a bump. George's tone grew serious when he mentioned his expectations for Willow. "I want Willow to focus on her studies. Relationships are good, but education has to come first." His words hung in the air.

William felt a twinge of anxiety. *Was he just a distraction?*

Mama chimed in, "I get where yah comin' from, George. Education's important, but so are friendships. They build character, don't they?"

Papa nodded thoughtfully, adding, "Life is a balance, isn't it?"

Slowly, the weight lifted, and Ava suggested a game to lighten the mood. "How about a scavenger hunt in the forest?" The idea sparked instant excitement, and everyone eagerly jumped up to explore.

The forest turned into an adventure. Parents and kids alike laughed as they searched for hidden treasures like colorful stones and odd twigs.

William felt a wave of relief; the distance between the adults seemed to shrink with every laugh.

As they returned to the picnic area, the atmosphere was lighter. George smiled at William, nodding approvingly. "Yah've got a good head on yoah shoulders. Keep it up." The compliment felt like a triumph.

That day by the forest's edge became more than just a picnic; it became a bridge between families. By the time they packed up, William no longer worried about George's approval. They'd shared laughter, stories, and a meal, and they all felt a little closer.

Part VII: The Tarn's Promise

"Yah won't catch a thing with that line," William taunted, watching Willow cast into the still waters of the tarn. Strands of hair had slipped from her loose bun, framing her face with a softness that made him smile.

"Oh, hush," Willow shot back, her eyes flashing with a spark of playful defiance. "Yah just don't have the patience." The earthy scent of dew lingered in the air, mingling with a faint trace of campfire smoke. William's gaze lingered on Willow, feeling their connection deepen with each shared moment.

They'd been friends for years, neighbors in Tasmania's rugged countryside, but now their bond felt as vivid as the red waratahs blooming along the bank.

A tug on her line broke the silence. Willow laughed, lifting a glinting trout. "See? I didn't need fancy fishin' skills after all."

Her laughter filled the air, a melody William knew he'd never tire of. She unhooked the fish, placing it into their wooden bucket. William took a breath, his heart racing, he reached for her hand. "Willow, will yah marry me?"

When she gazed into his eyes, all she found was sincerity. "Yes, William."

The two embrace and share a passionate kiss which was interrupted by the sound of approaching hoof beats. George smiled as he dismounted, approval clear in his eyes. "Ava and I knew you two were destined for this."

He unrolled a parchment. "Here—500 acres, with the tarn. To start a life togetha."

That evening, they shared the news with Mama and Papa, hands clasped as stars winked above them. Wedding preparations soon filled their days, the joyful sounds and plans echoing across the tarn.

On their wedding day, families gathered by the water. Tables were laden with scallop pie, roast lamb, and fresh-baked bread.

After the vows, George and Ava gifted a small herd of Herdwick sheep. William and Willow looked into each other's eyes, knowing this was just the beginning.

That night, as moonlight danced across the tarn, Willow whispered, "Thank yah faw choosin' me."

William replied, "Thanks for sayin' yes. This is our place now—our tarn, our land, our life."

Part VIII: Where New Roots Take Hold

Their life together waited like an unwritten story, a journey they were eager to begin. For now, they would live separately until their home was ready.

William worked alongside his father, adding delicate details to the furniture they'd started earlier from the sturdy cider gum. Wood shavings curled to the floor, blending with the tree's tangy scent as William carefully carved intricate designs into the wood.

The most precious piece was the baby crib. William's heart swelled as he worked, imagining the tiny form that would rest within it. When he smoothed the last edge with his palm, he felt the wood's warmth and the promise it held.

The house took months to build, each day blending into a blur of labor and sweet anticipation. It would be a simple abode, but it would be theirs.

When the last touches were complete, they crossed the threshold together, sunlight breaking over their new beginning.

They grew their sheep farm together, each complementing the other's strengths—his strategy, her tenderness with animals. Their flock thrived, and their wool grew thick and strong, earning a good reputation in the community.

One evening, as they sat on the porch with their legs dangling, William turned to Willow. "It's time. We have enough to start our family."

"Are yah sure?"

He nodded, squeezing her hand. "More than anythin'."

A few months later—the harvest season in full bloom—they sold the best of their flock. The money exchanged was more than they'd ever seen—a tangible reward for their hard work and commitment to each other.

That night, Willow felt the first flutter of new life beneath her hand. The land had given them a home and a life, and now it seemed it would give them a family.

One evening, Mama came by with a basket of herbs, her knowledge filling the room with warmth. She led Willow to a quiet corner, the scents of rosemary and sage following like a comforting embrace.

With a gentle touch, Mama tied a simple wedding band to a string, holding it over Willow's rounded belly. She watched it sway. "It's a boy," she murmured, her voice rich with certainty. "See how it moves, like the tail of a young fox? He'll be quick and cleva', like his fahthah."

Willow's hand rested on her belly, feeling the life within. "A boy," she whispered, letting the reality sink in.

Mama nodded, her gaze soft. "He'll have the strength of the wombat and the grace of the swan. He'll be a leada', this one."

William's heart filled with pride and a touch of nervousness. He imagined teaching his son the ways of the land and the value of hard work.

Mama placed a gentle hand on Willow's belly, her tone turning solemn. "But rememba', his spirit is wild. He must find his own path, even as yah guide him."

Willow grew more radiant as motherhood approached, and their preparations intensified. Beeswax candles filled the house, mingling with the earthy aroma of Mama's herbs.

When the first snow fell, Willow went into labor. It was a long, trying night, but with Mama's calm presence and William's steady hand, they welcomed their son into the world. The baby boy's cry echoed across the land, a declaration of new life.

Feeling a deep sense of responsibility, William planted a tree for his son, continuing the family tradition. He chose a spot on a gentle knoll where the earth felt alive beneath his feet, the tarn in the distance.

William knelt by the spot, pressing his hands into the soft soil as he guided the young Alpine Ash into place. His fingers felt the sapling's roots embrace the earth—an anchor, like the life he'd started to build.

A faint smile touched his lips. This tree was more than a symbol; it was a living connection to their land, a bridge between the past, present, and future.

"This tree, Henry, will be yoah life companion," he whispered. "It'll grow alongside yah, year by year, reachin' faw the sky. It'll witness yoah triumphs and heartaches, and one day, it'll guide yah."

This Alpine Ash, planted with hope, would root itself in the same soil that held their family's dreams. Later, as he gazed down at the tiny bundle in his arms, William knew their life together was just beginning. The tarn held their past, yet it was the land, the trees, and the very soil beneath them that would shape their future.

To this day, if you visit the central highlands, you might still see towering trees that will guide each Thompson's journey.

###

Romance/Folk Lore, Tasmania, Australia

*The spark for this story is from my love of the Australian accent. Period. I feel like when an Australian speaks—with your eyes closed—you'd feel as if the speaker had a smile on their face. The Irish–I feel the same way about them.

The Alchemist's Folly

THE FIRST ENCOUNTER WAS swift and brutal. An acidic snowball whizzed past Freya's head, sizzling as it hit a tree behind her—a razor-sharp reminder of the danger they faced.

Desperate villagers fought back, eagerly assaulting the snowmen. Despite their fear, they fought as a ragtag front united against the advancing evil.

The battle was pure chaos. Screams pierced the air, and the snowmen hissed with rage as they lunged forward, their acidic forms melting the snow into streaks of green sludge.

Boots skidded on slime as the villagers weaved past the monsters' grasp, careful not to brush against their deadly touch.

Freya knew they couldn't win this war without finding the source. As she dodged another snowball, something metallic caught her eye—a glint of glass and steel amid the frozen wreckage. *Is it the old legend? The one Malachai used to tell about the alchemist who tried to trap souls in snow? The chamber.*

Malachai had warned the children never to build snowmen near the old woods. "Some snow remembers," he'd mutter. Most laughed. Freya never did.

"This way!" she shouted, pointing toward the shimmering object. The villagers rallied around her, their spirits lifted at the glimpse of a potential end. Now they were ready to end the curse that had twisted snowmen into monsters.

The air stung—each breath burned like bleach. The acid snowmen left a wake of scorched snow and rust-laced fumes. Worse, with every minute they neared the chamber, new snowmen clawed up from the ice, their forms bubbling with unnatural life.

The entrance loomed: a dark slit in the mountainside. The metal door was pocked with acidic scars, almost eaten through in places. Freya halted mid-step. Her chest rose with sharp, shallow breaths.

Behind her, more snowmen emerged from the fog. Their eyes gleamed with malice. The temperature dropped, and the acidic air stung their lungs. Still, no one turned back.

"We're close," she murmured, steadying herself.

As Freya stepped forward, a memory flickered—a child's laughter, a mother's soft smile. *They're gone. Gone to the acid. But I can't let their deaths be for nothing.* Her sister had screamed from the attic window, clutching their baby brother, as the snowmen melted through the roof. Freya hadn't reached them in time.

With a deep breath, she crossed the threshold. Her companions followed.

"Will we make it, Freya?" a young man whispered, his voice trembling.

"We don't have a choice," she said, eyes fixed ahead. "We either end this now... or lose everything." *What if I'm wrong? What if I can't stop this?* She glanced back. Faces worn, bleeding, burned—but filled with trust. *I can't let them down.*

The air inside the chamber tasted metallic, sharp as knives. Their footsteps echoed as they ventured deeper, the floor cracking like brittle bone beneath their boots.

At the center of the chamber stood a giant pulsing crystal, its sickly green light bathing the twisted machinery around it. The snowmen's birthplace.

Freya felt its hostility—not just magic, but something alive and aware, pushing against her presence like a heartbeat that wasn't hers.

Malachai's voice broke the silence. "Long ago, a reclusive alchemist lived beyond the village. Known for dabbling with life and death."

Freya turned to him. "Are we in his lair?"

"It smells like it. He bound life into snow hoping for eternal youth. An elixir. What he made was acid and death."

"In his mind winter held a perfect stillness—immortality in its silence," Malachai added. "But his formula corrupted it. Life can't bloom in poison."

The crystal glowed brighter as they neared. Snowmen poured in from hidden crevices in the walls, surrounding them.

Their hissing grew deafening.

The villagers closed ranks, forming a protective circle around Freya.

Weapons clutched, eyes wide, jaws clenched. She stepped closer to the crystal.

It pulsed in time with her heartbeat. Cold—colder than ice—and yet it burned. Her hand trembled as she touched it. She didn't pull away.

Malachai once said: "Every curse has a heart. Crush the heart, and the curse dies with it."

She shut her eyes. Focused. Searched for weakness. The surrounding noise faded until nothing remained but the pulse—the crystal's breath. Warmth stirred inside her. Faint at first. Then stronger. *Hope.*

The snowmen shrieked, flailing wildly. They felt it too—the shift, the unraveling.

With a cry, Freya slammed her hand into the crystal.

A thunderous crack split the air. Shards burst outward in a blinding flash.

The chamber fell silent when the crystal shattered.

The snowmen let out one last hiss before collapsing into sludge. A rotting stench curled from the ground, like the afterbirth of something ancient. Something that had been decaying long before their time.

Mouths hung open. Weapons clattered to the floor. No one spoke.

The acid snowfall stopped.

Outside, the sky shifted. Clean snow fell—pure, white, gentle. It covered the battle's scars like a blessing.

Their village will heal.

Exhausted, the survivors walked back in silence. Only the crunch of snow beneath their feet broke the stillness.

The monsters that terrorized them were nothing more than puddles now, steaming in the cold.

As they reached the outskirts of the village, the sun pierced through the clouds in a sliver. A promise.

"This story will be told for generations," someone said.

"The alchemist thought he created eternal life," Malachai said. "His experiment went wrong."

He paused, his eyes glinting.

"Instead, he made monsters. Acid-filled snowmen who devoured everything in their path. He disappeared, leaving devastation. I told this tale to every child born in this village for the last hundred years."

A few villagers looked at him sideways.

Some whispered later that Malachai had found the alchemist's elixir himself. But no one asked him outright.

Not after what they'd seen.

And deep beneath the snow, a single shard of green crystal pulsed—once, faintly.

Then again.

Speculative Fiction

Silent Famine

THE SUN WAS JUST shining through the office windows at the B.E.E.S. headquarters. Agent Rae tapped her earpiece. Listening intently to the buzz of encrypted signals.

It was only fitting that a world-saving bee squad started the day before dawn. In those early hours before chaos reached them.

With her backpack slung over one shoulder, Rae maneuvered around crates filled with hives recovered the night before.

For the Bee Ecosystem Enforcement Services Squad (B.E.E.S. Squad), each mission was another line of defense in an invisible war.

Meanwhile, across the sprawling city on the brink of dawn, Alec moved with the grace of a shadow through quiet alleyways.

His eyes, a piercing shade of blue, scanned the dim streets, searching for signs of life amid ivy-covered ruins.

The buzz of distant machinery mingled with the scent of rain-soaked earth. His hand rested lightly on the stun gun at his side, ready for action.

Unlike Rae's squad, Alec preferred working alone. His mission was clear: locate the stolen hives, neutralize the traffickers, and ensure the bees' safe return.

Back at HQ Rae analyzed the fresh data sent by Dex, the team's ethical hacker. Dex reported, his voice steady despite the urgent situation, "We've found significant activity in the southern greenhouse district. Alec is already in the field, and thermal imaging suggests traffickers are active."

"Copy that," Rae replied. "Team, suit up. We're heading to Alec's location."

The faint hum Alec heard at the city's edge intensified, becoming a low thrum that vibrated through his body.

The rusty door of an abandoned greenhouse creaked open as he approached, revealing dim solar lamps that cast an eerie glow inside.

The makeshift hives and the buzzing of the agitated bees proved his suspicions right: this was a large-scale black-market enterprise.

His heart pounded as he witnessed a beekeeper awkwardly moving bees into smaller containers. The thief's actions screamed of desperation and greed.

Alec stepped forward, the crunch of glass underfoot giving him away. "B.E.E.S. Squad!" he barked. "Drop the bees and come with me."

The thief froze, but Alec's instincts screamed *danger*. The figure's hand hovered near a button that could release the bees in a chaotic swarm.

Alec steadied his stun gun, ready for the worst. At the same moment, Rae and her team arrived outside the greenhouse.

Through her infrared goggles, Rae spotted Alec's tense standoff with the trafficker. "We've got Alec inside," Rae whispered into her comms. "Form a perimeter and prepare for extraction. We stick to the Pollinator Protocol. The hives come first—always."

Inside, Alec wrestled with the weight of the moment. He knew it wasn't just about the bees in this greenhouse—it was about every hive they represented.

Without bees, the fields surrounding the city would soon turn barren.

Crops would fail, and the ripple effect would devastate the global food chain.

He'd seen it before in other places, and the memory of those hollowed-out towns haunted him.

Alec tensed as the thief lunged, swinging the container of bees wildly. He fired his stun gun, the crackle of electricity cutting through the hum of wings.

The figure crumpled to the ground, but the bees were already agitated. Alec moved swiftly, securing the container and calming the nearest hives as best he could.

Rae and her squad burst through the greenhouse door, their movements fluid and practiced. "Good timing," Alec said, his voice steady despite the adrenaline coursing through him.

"Always," Rae replied, her team already moving to secure the stolen hives.

Drones equipped with genetic trackers flitted between the crates, scanning and cataloging the precious bees. Dex's voice crackled through their comms, confirming the data upload.

As Rae's squad moved the hives, Alec caught a glimpse of figures in the shadows—rival traffickers, their faces obscured by makeshift masks.

Their sharp, purposeful movements hinted at military precision, fueling Alec's unease.

"Another trafficking group is nearby," Dex warned. "Very well armed."

"Understood," Rae said, exchanging a glance with Alec. "We need to move quickly."

As Rae moved through the greenhouse, she thought of her family's orchard. She could still remember her father walking through the almond groves, his calloused hands brushing over barren blossoms. "We've lost another acre, Rae," he'd said, his voice breaking in a way she'd never heard before.

The look in his eyes—a man already mourning a future he wouldn't live to see—was the reason she was here now, leading this fight.

Alec noticed her hesitation. "You okay?" he asked quietly.

"Just thinking about what happens if we lose," Rae said, her voice hardening. "If the bees disappear."

Alec nodded. He didn't need her to explain. The stakes had been driven into him long ago. He didn't talk much about his past, but there was a reason he worked alone.

Once, he'd trusted someone else in the field. He could still hear his partner's screams and see the chaos as a swarm unleashed by traffickers tore through Alec's team. That day had taught him a bitter truth: trust was dangerous.

Together, they worked to extract the hives. Rae's team calmed the bees with precision tools while Alec kept watch for any sign of the rival crew.

The rustling of leaves and distant footsteps sent shivers down their spines, but the extraction went off without a hitch.

Back at headquarters, Rae and Alec stood side by side, watching Dex analyze the recovered data. "We're getting better at this," Dex said, his voice tinged with optimism. "The B.E.E.S. Squad is saving more bees every day."

Rae nodded, her gaze drifting to the map of hotspots. "One day, we'll put an end to this black market," she said softly. "Until then, we keep fighting."

Alec didn't say much.

But as he looked at the rescued hives, a rare smile flickered across his face.

They call us the Guardians of the Hive, but sometimes it feels like the hive is guarding us—keeping the world alive one pollination at a time.

###

Eco-Thriller

The Incident in Room 629

SARAH HAD ALWAYS BEEN a skeptic. Ghost stories, paranormal activity, things that go bump in the night. She dismissed them all with an eye roll.

Standing at Room 629 in the Overlook Hotel, she felt something was terribly, horribly wrong. It had started innocently enough. A weekend getaway to the mountains, a chance to clear her head after a messy breakup.

The Overlook seemed perfect–isolated, peaceful, with breathtaking views of the Rockies. The off-season rates were a steal.

The first signs of trouble came during check-in. The elderly clerk's hands shook as he handed over the key, his rheumy eyes darting nervously to the brass number attached to an old-fashioned key chain. "Are you sure you want 629?"

Sarah kept her original booking. She'd read about Room 629 online. It was supposed to be one of the most haunted rooms in the country. Part of her had chosen it as a challenge to her own disbelief.

As floorboards creaked ominously beneath her feet, Sarah regretted her bravado.

Inserting the key, she winced at the echoing click. The door swung open with a groan that set Sarah's teeth on edge.

The room was unremarkable–dingy wallpaper, velvet drapes, a four-poster bed that had seen better days. As her eyes adjusted to the gloom, her skin crawled.

Dark stains, like old blood, on the carpet. Scratch marks on the bedposts, as if something–or someone–had clawed in desperation. And everywhere, a faint, sickly sweet smell reminiscent of decay.

Sarah shook her head, trying to dispel the growing unease. It was just an old room, nothing more. Her imagination was working overtime, fueled by too many late-night horror movies and creepy pasta stories.

The large, claw-foot tub dominated the space, its white enamel dulled from age. Sarah ran her hand along the rim, shuddering at how icy cold the cast iron felt beneath her fingers.

As she turned, for a split second, she thought she saw the reflection of an old woman standing in the bathtub. Her gray hair plastered to her skull, her bloated face frozen in a silent scream.

Sarah whirled around, but the tub was empty.

There's no such thing as ghosts.

Sarah found it increasingly difficult to cling to her skepticism. She tried to distract herself by reading, but the words swam before her eyes, rearranging themselves into sinister messages:

"GET OUT"

"SHE'S COMING"

"ROOM 629 CLAIMS ANOTHER"

Sarah slammed the book shut. This was ridiculous. She was a grown woman, for crying out loud. There had to be a rational explanation for everything she was experiencing.

Sarah drew a hot bath to calm her nerves. She ran the taps, watching as steaming water filled the old tub.

The pipes groaned and sputtered, but Sarah attributed it to the hotel's aging plumbing. She stepped into the bath with a sigh of relief, sinking down into the soothing warmth.

She closed her eyes, letting the steam envelop her like a comforting blanket. But then, ever so slowly, she became aware of a change in the water.

It was getting colder.

Sarah's eyes snapped open.

The bathwater, which had been nearly scalding just moments ago, was now frigid.

Her breath came out in visible puffs, the temperature in the room plummeting.

And then she felt it—icy fingers wrapping around her ankles, pulling her down.

Sarah thrashed wildly, water splashing over the sides as she fought. She grasped the edges of the bathtub, her knuckles white with the effort of holding on.

"No! This isn't real."

But the hands were relentless, their grip tightening, nails digging into her flesh. Sarah could feel herself slipping, being dragged deeper into the impossible depths of the bathtub.

With a final, desperate surge of strength, she hauled herself out of the water, collapsing onto the cold tile floor. She scrambled to her feet, not even bothering with a towel.

She yanked at the exit but it wouldn't budge. The key, which she left in the lock, was gone.

She was trapped.

A low chuckle emanated from the bathroom, followed by the slow, methodical sound of wet footsteps. Sarah pressed herself against the far wall, her eyes fixed on the bathroom door as it creaked open.

The old woman from the mirror stood in the doorway, water cascading from her sodden nightgown. Her skin was a sickly gray-green, bloated and peeling in places.

Empty eye sockets stared at Sarah, a grotesque parody of a smile stretching across the specter's face.

"Welcome to Room 629, my dear," the apparition rasped, her voice like sandpaper on bone. "We've been waiting for you."

Sarah screamed, the sound tearing from her throat as the spirit lurched forward. She squeezed her eyes shut, bracing for the icy touch of death.

And then, silence.

Sarah opened her eyes.

The room was empty, no sign of the hideous specter. The bathroom door was closed, the floor dry. Even the scratch marks on the bedposts had vanished.

Sarah hoped it had all been a terrible nightmare. But then she caught sight of her reflection in the mirror.

Angry red marks circled her ankles where the grip of death had her. And just visible at the edge of her hairline was a single strand of long, gray hair that wasn't her own.

Sarah's scream echoed through the empty halls of the Overlook, but no one came to help. In Room 629, no one ever did.

The next morning, the elderly clerk shuffled towards Room 629, key in hand. Another guest had failed to check out. Another guest had failed to check out. Another accident.

The room was immaculate, no sign of the previous night's kerfuffle. The clerk's gaze fell on the bathroom door, ajar.

"I should've tried harder to warn her."

The clerk heard quiet laughter coming from the bathtub. He didn't look back.

Room 629 would be ready for its next victim soon enough.

*The spark for this story came from the number 217 being stuck in my head. I wrote a haunted hotel story, but changed the room number to 629. 629 was my clock number from 1989 when I worked in a sewing factory. Later, after I looked at this story with fresh eyes I learned that room 217 was connected to a King novel. Which is odd because I don't read his books, and didn't recall watching the movie with that number–until now.

Revenge a la Frostbite

Revenge à la Frostbite

Serves: 1 deserving individual
Preparation Time: Years in the making
Ingredients:
1 cup of grudges, finely minced
2 tablespoons of silent resentment
3 ounces of patience, aged to perfection
1 tablespoon of biting wit
A dash of indifference
1 ounce of kindness (optional, for garnishing)
Ice cubes of frozen opportunities

Instructions:
Prepare Your Mind Set your emotional temperature to "frozen." This dish is best prepared with a cold heart and your emotions have settled into an icy calm.

Combine Ingredients In a large bowl, mix the grudges with silent resentment. Stir until they meld together into a thick, unyielding paste.

Add Patience Fold in the aged patience, taking care not to rush. The longer the mixture rests, the more potent the flavor of revenge will be. Cover with plastic wrap and let it marinate in the darkest corner of your thoughts for several months or until it ripens.

Season With Wit Sprinkle in the biting wit, adding flavor to what might otherwise be too bitter to swallow. Ensure each barb is evenly distributed, enhancing the potency of the final dish.

Serve Cold Pour the mixture over ice cubes made from frozen opportunities. The colder, the better—the key to making revenge truly irresistible is its icy nature.

Garnish and Present Add a hint of kindness if desired, just enough to throw them off guard. Serve on a platter of indifference, making sure the edges are sharp.

Enjoy, but Beware: This dish often has a bitter aftertaste. Some have found that savoring it leaves them emptier than before. Consume with caution.

Written as a Recipe, Writing Exercise

The Tides of Freedom

THE SUN BEAT DOWN, turning the sidewalks into strips of white-hot concrete. Tina trudged home from another grueling day at the factory, her faded dress sticking to her skin.

Her eyes, once full of hope, now held only the dullness of long hours and her supervisor's sneering words.

Each step reminded her of the life she led, a far cry from the vibrant, adventurous world she longed for—the world of heroes and rebels from her favorite movies.

As she passed a dusty storefront, her eyes caught a glimpse of a familiar poster. There he was—Johnny Depp as Captain Jack Sparrow, that mischievous grin promising adventure on the open seas.

Her heart fluttered, warmth spreading through her as his image teased the life she dared not dream about.

Tina's lips twitched into a faint smile as she neared her apartment building—a towering, gray block that symbolized everything that suffocated her. Laughter drifted from a nearby park, a bitter reminder of the joy she rarely felt. For a brief moment, hope flickered inside her. Maybe there was still a way out of this suffocating existence.

She unlocked the door to her small, bare apartment, its emptiness a reflection of her own weary spirit. A single poster of Depp adorned the wall, faded but somehow still alive with possibility. She allowed herself to indulge in a fleeting fantasy—what if she were a pirate queen, standing beside him on the deck of a ship, wild and free?

Weeks passed, and her secret daydreams about Johnny Depp grew stronger, sustained by late-night movies and stolen glances at the posters.

Then one evening, as she stepped outside for air, she saw a man leaning against a lamppost, a cigarette dangling from his lips. He wore a tricorn hat and boots that looked out of place in her drab neighborhood.

Tina froze. The man raised his head, and her breath caught in her throat.

"Looking for someone?" he asked, amusement dancing in his eyes.

She stared, heart pounding. "Johnny Depp?"

He grinned, a flash of white in the dim light. "In the flesh," he replied with a bow. "But you can call me Captain Jack."

As they talked, Tina's shyness melted away. His stories of adventures and freedom soothed her weary soul, and she laughed more that night than she had in months.

He was everything she had dreamed of—charming, daring, and startlingly real.

Their meetings became frequent, each one drawing her deeper into his world.

They shared stories, secrets, and dreams, often sitting on the stoop of her building late into the night.

Tina started falling for him, swept up in his charm and the thrill of being noticed. But a voice in the back of her mind whispered that it was all too good to be true.

One night, as they sat close together, their hands brushed. A jolt shot through her, and she pulled back, flustered.

Johnny smirked, leaning in closer. "You've got a fire in you," he said softly. "We could set the world ablaze together."

Tina's heart raced. She knew the truth—she was just an ordinary girl, stuck in a mundane life. But with him, she felt alive.

When he finally asked her to leave it all behind and sail into the unknown, she didn't hesitate.

She packed her meager belongings into a worn satchel, casting one last glance at the gray walls she was leaving behind.

***

Their journey was wild, every moment with Johnny an adventure. They dodged bounty hunters, found hidden coves, and laughed as they stole kisses in the shadows. Tina learned to wield a sword, to navigate the waves, and with each passing day, she shed more of her old life.

She was becoming someone new—someone strong, fearless.

But the past, as it often does, threatened their happiness. Rival pirates hunted them, and with each battle, the danger grew.

Yet, even as they faced death together, Tina knew she'd never felt more alive.

It was her quick thinking that saved them in the end. Spotting a rogue current, she shouted for the crew to steer into it, and they escaped their enemies, emerging victorious.

As they anchored near an island rumored to hold treasure, Tina realized that what she sought wasn't gold or jewels, but the freedom she'd found alongside Johnny.

He adjusted his hat as the salty air filled his lungs, invigorating him. He and Tina stood before the ancient temple, its weathered stones etched with symbols.

"Look at those carvings," Tina said, pointing to a faded glyph. "They tell a story. Do you feel it? It's like the stones are alive."

Johnny grinned. "Let's see what secrets they hold." Together, they pushed aside the heavy vines that clung to the entrance.

A musty smell greeted them as they stepped inside, the dim light revealing crumbling walls adorned with more carvings.

They traversed the narrow corridor, reaching a grand chamber. The ceiling soared high, and in the center stood a pedestal. On it lay an old, weathered canvas scroll.

"Is that what I think it is?" Tina whispered, eyes wide with excitement.

Johnny unfurled it, tracing the delicate lines with his fingers. "The Fountain of Youth. It's real."

Tina gasped. "But it's a myth!"

"Myths have roots in truth, don't they?" Johnny's eyes sparkled.

They studied the map. It showed a path through treacherous mountains and dense jungles. "We have to go after it," Johnny said. "Think of what we may find."

Tina considered the risks. "But what if it's dangerous?"

"Every treasure hunt is dangerous," he replied. "But this... this could change everything."

With a determined nod, Tina agreed. They set out at dawn, the map guiding them through winding trails and thick foliage. They faced insects, wild animals, and even a rival crew of pirates who sought the fountain for themselves.

As they sat by the campfire, Tina poked the flames. "What if the fountain doesn't grant us eternal youth? What if it's a regular spring?"

Johnny tossed a twig into the fire. "Then we'll have an adventure worth telling. Besides, I'd rather chase a dream than sit idle."

***

They emerged from the jungle, standing before the fountain. It sparkled in the sunlight, surrounded by vibrant flowers. The air felt electric.

"Are we doing this?"

Johnny nodded, his heart racing. "Together."

They approached the fountain, the water shimmering like liquid crystal. Johnny cupped his hands, scooping some into his palms. "Cheers," he said, raising his hands.

"Cheers," Tina echoed.

They drank the cool water, which was invigorating. For a moment, time stood still. They laughed and splashed each other.

But as the sun set, something shifted. Johnny looked at Tina. "Do you feel different?"

She frowned. "No. What if it's a trick?"

"What if it's not about the water but about the journey?"

Tina smiled, relief washing over her. "You're right. We've lived more in these weeks than most do in a lifetime."

They stood together, realizing the adventure had changed them.

With the map tucked away, they turned back toward the path, knowing that life was the greatest adventure.

The final stretch of their journey was fraught with peril. The sea grew restless, waves towering like walls determined to block their path. Yet, Tina stood at the helm, her hand in Johnny's, her eyes locked on the horizon.

They weren't just pirates anymore—they were legends.

With a final glance at the island, they set sail again, their spirits unbroken. "Where to next?" she asked.

Johnny grinned. "To the ends of the Earth, and beyond."

###

Fan Fiction
*The spark for this story is from my appreciation of Johnny Depp's talent.

Pillars of Strength

"*¿Estás segura?* Are you sure, mamá?" Marisol's voice quivered as she clutched her mother's hand tightly, her wide eyes reflecting the weight of the unknown.

"*Sí,*" Pilamar reassured her, though her voice held the tremor of fear she tried to suppress. I have to stay strong—for her. "*Todo estará bien.* Everything will be fine."

They arrived at the meeting point, a desolate spot beside the dusty road. The setting sun cast an orange glow over the barren landscape. Her hands trembled, and she struggled to steady her breath. A tattered cargo van rattled up, its engine hissing like a coiled serpent ready to strike.

El Jefe, the driver, stepped out, his mustache twitching beneath a low-pulled baseball cap. He barked at the huddled group of migrants, "*¿Tienes el dinero?* Have money?"

Pilamar's hands trembled as she handed over the last of her savings. The wad of cash felt heavy in her palm—heavy with the weight of everything she had left. She dared not look at El Jefe, her gaze locked instead on the promise of Texas, a dream of a better and safer life for her daughter, Marisol.

The younger coyote, Chico, had neck tattoos, and the stature of a bear put his hand on Pilamar's buttocks, pushing her into the van. The interior was cramped, filled with the sour smell of fear and sweat.

Pilamar's heart raced as she squeezed into the back, and Marisol snuggled close to her side. El Jefe slammed the door shut, and the engine roared to life. The van lurched forward.

But the journey had barely begun when the tension mounted.

Two coyotes, Chico and Ramon, argued in furious grunts. Their voices rose above the hum of the engine. Ramon, frustrated with Chico's unwanted advances on Pilamar, scolded him. "Knock it off!"

Chico sneered, his teeth flashing in the fading light. "Or what?" he challenged, his lip quivering with anger. "You gonna make me?" There was a fierceness in Chico's stance—a cocky tilt to his head—that spoke of the power he wielded in this group. But he had to make sure everyone knew who was in charge.

Ramon didn't answer. The threat was clear in his stance. He stepped between Chico and Pilamar, his muscles taut. The woman's eyes grew wide with fear, but she remained silent.

The tension grew.

The air thickened with it.

Chico lunged. His fist connected with Ramon's jaw with a sickening crack. Chico—the one with the scar running from his right ear to the corner of his mouth—clamped onto Pilamar's wrist, fueling the argument.

Her heart skipped a beat.

She turned to face the towering, sweaty brute. Red threads marbled his eyes, fracturing the whites like lightning across a night sky. The sight sent a cold shiver down her spine, and she instinctively pulled back.

Ramon snatched Chico by the shoulder and drove a fist into his jaw, but the blow barely registered. Chico shoved him hard; Ramon slammed against the van's metal wall and crumpled, unconscious.

El Jefe turned his head around, and his eyes narrowed. "*No más,* Chico," he warned, his voice low and menacing.

The situation continued to spiral out of control as Chico returned his focus to Pilamar. Her mind raced as she struggled to break free. The memories of her past were a blur, but one thing was clear: *she wouldn't let history repeat itself.* She gathered all her strength and headbutted him with everything she had. There was a crunch, and the man's grip loosened.

The other passengers shifted uncomfortably, their gazes fixed firmly on the floor. A middle-aged man traveling with his wife rose to his feet, placing himself between Pilamar and Chico. El Jefe's grip on the steering wheel tightened. "*No hagas estupideces*—don't do anything stupid."

Chico laughed, his eyes gleaming with malice. He unsheathes his knife and drives the butt-end into the man's head. The man, crumpling onto the van floor unconscious, streamed blood from his wound. "*¿Por qué no?* Why not?"

"Reyes will not like this!"

He turns back to Pilamar. "Where were we?" His voice was a sinister purr.

Marisol, no more than ten years old, stepped forward, her small frame trembling but resolute. "*Déjala en paz*, leave her alone," she screamed, her voice echoing in the cramped space. The van swerved as El Jefe tried to regain control. The other passengers turned their faces away from the chaos, knowing their only salvation was to remain silent and unseen.

The van screeched to a halt. The back door burst open, and a gust of hot desert wind rushed in. Chico yanked Pilamar out into the desert. Dust swirled around them, obscuring their view.

Years of suppressed fear surged within her. She yanked her arm away and delivered a swift kick to his shin. The man howled in pain and surprise, but it only enraged him further. He lunged at her, his massive frame moving with surprising speed.

El Jefe went inside the van and shook Ramon to bring him around. "Chico! Get in."

For a moment, there was silence. And then Chico turned and lunged at her, his eyes gleaming with malice. But Pilamar's expression had changed. The fear is missing, replaced by something much colder.

Pilamar's instincts kicked in. She sidestepped and used her elbow to hit him in the gut. *He was too big and too strong.* He grabbed her by the hair and pulled her closer, his breath hot and nauseating in her face.

Pilamar's daughter followed, tears streaking her cheeks. "Mamá!" she cried, her voice trembling with fear. Before she reached her mother, Chico grabbed her by the arm and tossed her aside like a rag doll. She hit the ground hard. The wind knocked out of her.

The man who had tried to protect them lay motionless on the van floor, his wife cradling his head in her lap. Her eyes shut tight, and she sobbed. The rest of the passengers remained frozen in shock, unable to tear their eyes from the horror unfolding before them.

El Jefe woke Ramon, and he groaned and pushed himself up onto his elbows. Shaking off the daze in his head he got to his feet.

The scar on Chico's right cheek twisted as he leered at Pilamar, his intentions clear. He shoved her to the ground. Darkness closed in as Pilamar realized what was coming. Her mind raced for an escape. *She was no match for Chico's freakish brute strength.*

The world around her darkened. *No, not this.* Chico loomed above her, a predator. The force of Pilamar's heartbeat reverberated inside her ears. It deafened her to her screams. The smell of his unwashed clothes and the stench of alcohol on his breath hit her like a punch to the gut.

It was the same smell she had come to dread in her childhood home—the scent of her father after a night of binge-drinking, right before he unleashed his rage on her mother.

Pilamar's chest tightened, and she felt the world around her spin. Memories of her mother's cries echoed in her mind. In a gruff voice, slurred by alcohol, Chico demanded, "*Dame lo que quiero,* Give me what I want." He sneered, his breath hot and foul.

Pilamar's eyes narrowed, and she clenched her fists. *I'm not a scared little girl anymore. I'm a survivor. I'm a fighter.* She looked the man in the eye and said firmly, "*Déjame en paz,* Leave me alone."

But the man, fueled by his toxic mix of entitlement and liquor, didn't take the hint. He stumbled closer, his leering grin revealing yellowed teeth. "C'mon, don't be like that," he slurred, reaching out a meaty hand to touch her breast. The touch was like a match to gasoline.

Chico forced himself upon her, his weight pinning her to the hot sand. Panic overtook Pilamar as she struggled to break free, but her strength waned. *Chico is unphased. Unbothered. Unstoppable. Inhuman.*

Desperately, her hand scrambled through the sand, searching. *Anything—anything.* Her fingers brushed against something sharp. *A jagged rock.* With a surge of fury, she gripped it, gouged, and slashed. Creating a mirrored scar on his cheek was small, but so sweet revenge. She only heard the sounds of her daughter's sobs and the harsh, grunting noises coming from atop her.

Pilamar dug her fingers into the sand and filled both hands with gritty, red silt. Her pulse pounded as she shoved sand into Chico's eyes and the cut. She pressed the soil into Chico's open wound, the gritty particles biting into the raw flesh. Chico's body convulsed, a guttural howl ripping from his throat.

His eyes bulged wide with shock, and his hands flew to the wound, trying to claw the dirt away. But it was too late—each movement only ground the silt deeper into the gash, sending sharp waves of agony coursing through his body.

"You bitch!" Chico spat, his voice a strangulated mixture of rage and pain. He lunged at her, teeth bared like an animal, but his steps faltered, weakened by the searing discomfort radiating from the wound. Pilamar barely had time to leap back. Her heart was in her throat as Chico swung wildly at her. His strength and precision slipped with each passing second.

She could see it—*the way his fury blinded him, how the pain twisted his features into something monstrous.* She needed to keep him unbalanced, to stay unreachable until his rage burned itself out. *Come on, Pilamar. Keep moving. Don't let him catch you now.* She was shaking with adrenaline coursing through her veins, but she was alive.

For a moment, she stood there, watching him as he lay writhing and screaming in anguish, and gasped for a breath. Then, she turned on her heel and sprinted away from the scene, her heart hammering in her chest. She knew she wasn't safe yet, but she was free—free from the ghosts of her past and the clutches of a monster who threatened to pull her back into the darkness.

Pilamar, carrying her daughter, ran to the van in desperation. The coyotes threw them out of the group, leaving them with nothing but a half-empty water bottle and a loaf of stale bread. The passengers remained huddled in quiet, fearful clumps.

"*Camina*! Walk!" El Jefe called out, his voice cold and indifferent. "Andale!"

Ramon and El Jefe tossed Chico, still screaming in pain, into the van. The passengers sat in silence. *This woman who had stood up to the monster in their midst. They knew now she was not another face in the crowd, but someone to be feared and revered.* The engine roared to life again. The van disappeared into the distance, leaving only swirling dust in its wake. The scorched earth stretched endlessly before them.

When it was over, Pilamar lay there, broken and soiled, her soul feeling as barren as the desert surrounding them. The only solace was the feel of her daughter's tight grip around her waist. *¡Dios! ¿Por qué? God! Why?* They had been abandoned.

The promise of Texas is a distant mirage taunting them from afar. As the darkness fell, Marisol clung to her mother, whispering, "Mamá, *no llorés. Estaré contigo.* Don't cry. I'll be with you."

Pilamar felt the warmth of Marisol's body pressed against her own; the girl's trembling was a telltale sign of her fear. *Dios, por favor dame fuerzas, God, please give me strength. I have to survive.* With a deep breath and trembling arms Pilamar pushed herself to a sitting position. Her legs, still weak from the trauma, buckled as she attempted to stand.

The man's stench clung to her skin. The lack of water was a cruel mockery of her desperation to erase the evidence of his brutality. She looked around, searching for something, anything, to clean herself with.

Her gaze fell upon the patch of desert sand. The same sand that had witnessed her agony now offered the only means of purification she had. Wincing, she reached down and scooped a handful of the gritty granules. They felt alien against her tender flesh as she began to scrub at her body, trying to exorcise the memories along with the blood and sweat.

Each grain scraped her skin—a pain she could control. She continued with grim determination. The sand stung, but it was a pain she could bear, a pain she could understand, unlike the invisible wounds festering within her.

Her eyes stung with the effort not to cry, not to wake Marisol. She refused to let her daughter see her like this—broken and soiled. The thought of her little girl being exposed to such horror was unbearable. *She had to be strong, for Marisol.* With each scrape of the sand, Pilamar told herself she was one step closer to erasing the vile touch of the man who had stolen her dignity.

Her breaths came in shallow gasps as she worked, her mind racing with thoughts of escape and revenge. She knew she had to keep moving, keep surviving, for Marisol. The sand clung to her skin, mixing with the drying blood and sticky sweat, creating a paste that spoke of her desperation. Once she felt clean enough, Pilamar pulled the torn fabric of her dress back over her bruised body.

"Marisol. Wake up, sweetie. We must go." Marisol rubbed the sleep from her eyes. She stood and hugged her mama and sobbed. Pilamar ignored the urge to sob. "Come. No time for this." Pilamar knew the child had heard everything. *The sound of her mother's pain was something she'd never be able to scrub away.*

They walked for hours, the bread and water barely sustaining them. She berated herself for trusting those men. *How would they find their way through the desert now?* She focused on putting one foot in front of the other, her eyes searching the horizon for any sign of civilization.

Pilamar and Marisol found themselves alone. Pilamar scoured the ground for more sharp rocks, carefully selecting a few pieces for makeshift weapons. She placed a carefully selected rock in each of Marisol's pant pockets. "*Úsalo para protección. Como lo hice yo?* Use it for protection. Like I did."

Under the cold starlight, they began their painful journey on foot. They stumbled through the night, the cold ground a reminder of their new reality.

As dawn broke, the heat grew oppressive, and Pilamar tried to ration the water, but Marisol's pleas grew more insistent. The relentless sun blazed overhead as Pilamar and Marisol trudged through the arid landscape, their footsteps crunching on the cracked earth. The desert stretched before them, unforgiving sand and sparse vegetation.

Their mouths were parched, and their stomachs growled in protest. They had to find water—something to sustain them—until they made it out of this bleak place.

Marisol's voice, laced with desperation, broke the silence. "Mamá, *tengo mucha sed*, I'm so thirsty."

Pilamar glanced at Marisol, her heart aching at the sight of Marisol's dry, cracked lips. I need to act quickly. "We will find something," she reassured, scanning the horizon.

Her eyes fell upon a cluster of tall, spiny cacti a short-distance away. "There," she pointed. "Barrel cacti. *Almacenan agua*, They store water."

Approaching the cacti cautiously, Pilamar used the slate-shard makeshift knife to slice open the thick, waxy skin. Inside, the cactus revealed its fibrous flesh, a potential source of hydration.

"Careful," Pilamar warned. "*El agua de cactus puede enfermarnos si bebemos demasiado Toma sorbos pequeños*, Cactus water can make us sick if we drink too much. Take small sips."

She carefully extracted a small portion of the flesh, squeezing the pulp to release the water. The liquid was bitter, but it was something. Pilamar handed it to Marisol, who sipped tentatively, grimacing at the taste.

"Slow," Pilamar urged, taking a small sip herself. The liquid coated her throat, offering some relief but also a faint burn. "*No mucho.*"

With their immediate thirst slightly quenched, Pilamar knew they needed to press on and find a place to rest before the scorching afternoon sun reached its zenith. "We must keep moving."

They resumed their journey, Marisol's steps faltering but determined. She clutched Pilamar's hand as they trudged forward, eyes scanning for any sign of life. Each step felt heavier than the last, but Pilamar knew they couldn't stop now. They had to survive. They would survive.

Scanning the area, Pilamar spotted a cluster of prickly pear cacti not far from the barrel cacti. The flat pads, known as nopales, were edible if prepared correctly. They were covered in spines, but the bright red fruits, the tunas, could be eaten raw.

"*Recoge estas*, Collect these," Pilamar said, using her slate shard to remove the spines from the pads and fruits. The work was slow and painstaking, but they gathered enough for a small meal.

"Fire," Pilamar suggested, "makes it easier to digest."

They gathered dry brush and twigs to start a small fire with the matches Pilamar had tucked away in her socks. Pilamar skewered the pads and held them over the flames, roasting them until they were tender. They ate the raw fruits, savoring the sweet, juicy flesh.

Marisol bit into one of the roasted pads, her face lighting up with relief. It's not much, but it's better than nothing. Pilamar nodded, taking a bite herself. The nopales had a slightly tangy taste, but they were nourishing. It wasn't a feast, but it would keep them going.

***

Exhaustion took hold before noon. The relentless march of the sun mocked their progress. Pilamar's thoughts grew hazy, and she could feel her strength waning. The desert's unforgiving terrain tested their limits. But she had made a promise to Marisol—to keep fighting. So she did, despite the pain in her legs and the burning in her chest.

In the midday heat, they stumbled upon a dilapidated shack, a beacon of hope in the sea of sand and rock. They staggered inside, the darkness offering a brief reprieve from the sun's wrath. Inside, they found an old, glass jar filled with what looked like rainwater. They drank greedily, ignoring the metallic taste.

The floor beneath her was a cold, harsh reminder of the events which had unfolded the night before. She stared at the ceiling, noticing the cobwebs dancing in the corners, and wished she could pull one over her own reality. Pilamar's eyes fluttered from the unforgiving sun, the light piercing through the cracks in the shack's wooden slats. Her body felt like it had been trampled by a herd of wild horses, each muscle protesting as she attempted to move.

She knew she couldn't lie there forever. Marisol needed her. She shifted, her mind racing through the fog of pain and fatigue. *What if the coyotes returned?* The panic flickered inside her, but she shoved it down, gritting her teeth as she forced herself to sit up.

But the respite was short-lived.

As they rested, the sound of an approaching engine pierced the silence. Pilamar's heart leaped into her throat. She felt a fierce protectiveness surge through her. *Had the coyotes returned to finish what they had started? Or was it someone else, perhaps even more dangerous?*

She grabbed Marisol's hand and pulled her into the shadows, their eyes wide with fear. The rumble grew louder, and soon, a cloud of dust announced the arrival of a truck.

The door swung open, and a figure emerged. Pilamar squinted, trying to make out the silhouette in the blinding light. It was a woman, her face lined with the same adversity they had endured. She approached them slowly, her eyes filled with compassion. "*¿Necesitan ayuda?*, Need help?"

Pilamar felt a spark of hope flicker in her chest. Maybe, they had found an angel in this hellish place.

"*Sí, por favor*," she managed to croak out, her voice barely a whisper. "Our coyotes... they left us."

The stranger's expression softened, though a hint of anger remained. "I know the type," she said, her voice carrying a mix of sympathy and frustration. "But you're safe here."

"*Sí.*"

"I'm Martina. *Los bandidos nos robaron al grupo y me dejaron atrás,* Bandits robbed our group and abandoned me. *Sobrevivió rebuscando y estableciendo un campamento cerca de esta choza,* I survived by scavenging and setting up a camp near this shack." Her eyes searched their bruised and weary faces. "I have food and water." She offered it without another word.

As they ate, Martina spoke of her journey, her voice filled with determination. She had been traveling for weeks, hoping to find people desperate for help. The stories she shared were harrowing, but Pilamar found relief in the fact they weren't alone in their suffering.

With renewed energy, the three of them set out together, Martina leading the way with a confidence Pilamar hadn't seen in anyone for a long time. The desert was unforgiving, but Martina knew intimately—where to find water, which plants were safe to eat, and how to navigate the desert terrain.

The heat was relentless, and the cold of the night air bit into their bones. They saw no other signs of life, only the occasional buzzard, circling high above, a grim reminder of the fate awaiting the unfortunate.

But Pilamar found strength in Marisol's resilience and Martina's unyielding spirit. They became a makeshift family, sharing their fears and their dreams. And in the quiet moments, when the desert's whispers lulled them into a restless sleep, Pilamar swore she would never let anyone harm her daughter again.

Their journey was fraught with danger—snakes slithering in the shadows, the ever-present risk of dehydration, and the looming specter of Patrulla fronteriza, the Border Patrol. Yet, they pushed on, driven by hope and the fierce love binding them together. Before they abandoned the truck—out of gas and too risky to keep near the border checkpoints—they had gathered what little supplies they could carry, knowing the rest of their journey would be on foot.

The wind picked up, sending dust devils twirling across the landscape. A lone figure, Martina, emerged from the dust, her dark hair fluttering like a flag in the breeze. Behind her, two others, Pilamar and Marisol, trudged wearily, their footsteps dragging in the loose dirt.

The trio had met by chance at a shack far from the border, Martina, with her sharp instincts and unyielding spirit, had stepped up to guide them through the desert.

Pilamar glanced at Martina, admiring her perseverance, confidence, and vast knowledge of this unforgiving land. They had all lost so much, but here they were, pushing forward together.

Marisol, her shoulders stooped from the weight of her backpack, took a sip from her nearly empty water bottle. Her English was limited to the Basic English classes in Primaria, grade school, and what her parents taught her. She communicates her gratitude to Martina every so often.

As the first stars began to twinkle in the deepening blue sky, Martina called for a rest stop. They had to rest while they still had the light. She pointed out a cluster of rocks that could provide some shelter from the night's chill. "We'll camp here," Martina said, her voice firm but kind, as she knelt down, gathering twigs for the fire.

Pilamar and Marisol nodded, too tired to argue. They set about gathering firewood and preparing a meager meal of jerky and nuts. The fire crackled, casting flickering shadows across their faces. Martina knew they had a long way to go, and the desert held many secrets—some beautiful, some terrifying. But she had faced worse, and she wasn't about to let her new companions down.

As they sat in the tranquility of the desert night, she shared her survival knowledge, speaking in a blend of Spanish and English Marisol could understand. Pilamar listened intently, eager to learn from her experience.

Marisol, with her eyes downcast, spoke. "You... you're very strong, Martina," she said. "How do you learn this?"

"Survival is a teacher without mercy. You learn fast, or you don't learn at all." She paused, her gaze lingering on the horizon. "But it's not just about being strong. It's about knowing when to rest, when to push on, and when to trust your instincts."

Pilamar leaned in, his curiosity piqued. "What about the language, Martina?" she asked. "*¿Por qué crees que es importante que hablemos solo en inglés?* Why do you think it's important for us to speak only English?"

"English is the key to a new life in America," she said. "It's the language of opportunity. And if you and Marisol are going to make it there, you need to blend in, to be invisible. The less you stand out, the safer you'll be."

The conversation grew more personal as the embers of the fire burned low. Martina spoke of the moments that had shaped her into the woman she is today—the loss of her home, the death of her husband, and her relentless pursuit of a better life.

Martina, staring into the dying embers said, "I remember the night our house burned down. I stood outside, helpless, watching everything I had built go up in flames. My husband—he tried to save what he could, but…"

Pilamar spoke softly. "I'm sorry, Martina. It's hard to lose everything like that. I can't imagine. How did the fire start?"

Martina, nodding, eyes distant, "It was like watching my past disappear into smoke. And then losing him… it felt like the ground was pulled out from under me." The words faded into the horrific flashback.

Chapter II: Martina's Story

In the heart of a dusty Mexican village, Martina tended her garden like a saint. In a place often known only by hardship, the scent of marigolds filled the air—a small reminder that warmth and beauty could still bloom.

Joaquín, her ten-year-old son, darted from behind a tree, his laughter breaking the evening's calm. His dark chocolate eyes—so much like his mother's—sparkled with mischief as he charged toward her, a fistful of dirt in hand. Martina swatted at him.

From the house, Emilio, her husband, appeared, his face weary from the day's work. Yet, his eyes softened as he watched his wife and son. He called out, "Dinner is ready." Joaquín's laughter faded, and he dropped the dirt, knowing his mother's patience had limits.

Inside, the crackling fire joined the smell of beans and tortillas. Martina watched Emilio and Joaquín from the kitchen, her heart swelling with gratitude. Moments like these made the endless struggle of village life bearable.

A distant rumble of engines grew louder, shattering the peace. Martina panicked as she recognized the sound—motorcycles, the telltale sign of the cartel. Emilio's eyes darkened. Ushering them into the bedroom, he grabbed the shotgun hidden beneath their bed. "Hide," he urged in a whispered voice.

The thunder of boots soon followed, the vibrations trembling through the floor. Joaquín's grip tightened around Martina's hand as they huddled in the shadows. Outside, the night roared with engines and shouts. Then came the crash—the front door torn from its hinges, the room flooded with light as three cartel members barged in.

One grabbed Joaquín, yanking him from Martina's arms. She screamed, her cries silenced by a rough hand clamped over her mouth. From the darkness, Emilio stepped forward, his shotgun raised. "One step closer, and I'll blow your head off!" he warned, his voice shaking.

Reyes, the cartel leader, stepped into view, his cold eyes gleaming beneath his bandana. "Do you think you can stand against us?" he sneered. He gestured, and his men subdued Emilio.

Reyes lit a cigarette. The ember glowed ominously. "Where is it?" he demanded. "The package you've been hiding." Martina's heart sank. They had been careful while secretly distributing medical supplies to the village. But somehow the cartel discovered their activities.

The men ransacked the house, and it wasn't long before one returned, holding a small bag. Torn fabric revealed the smuggled supplies. Reyes' smile was cold. He nodded to his men, who began dousing the house in gasoline.

Martina and Emilio locked eyes, the understanding between them unmistakable—they had to save Joaquín. With a roar, Emilio lunged at Reyes, but the hail of bullets drowned out the shotgun blast. Emilio crumpled to the ground, lifeless.

The flames spread fast, and the smoke choked the air. Martina staggered to her feet, desperate to save her son. But through the thickening haze, she saw him dragged away, limp in the arms of one of the men. Her scream pierced the night.

Outside, the cartel mounted their motorcycles, with Joaquín slumped on the back of one. "You want him back?" Reyes taunted. "Then tell me where the rest is."

Martina's legs buckled. She fell to her knees, tears mixing with the sweat on her face. The fire consumed her home and village. She watched as the cartel disappeared into the night, the rumble of their engines fading into silence.

The stench of burning wood filled the air, mingling with the distant cries of her neighbors. Martina's heart felt as though it had shattered; the weight of her loss was nearly unbearable. But she had to move. She had to find Joaquín.

Martina stumbled through the village barefoot, her feet burning on the hot ground. She pushed through the chaos, through the swirling smoke and flames, her thoughts only on her son.

At the village's edge, she paused, knowing she needed help. Alone, she couldn't face the cartel. With a final glance at the smoldering ruins of her home, she turned toward the desert. "Guide me," she whispered to the stars above. "Guide me to him."

Her journey across the desert was relentless. The harsh sun cut through the sky, slicing her skin and drying her throat. Yet, she pressed on, determined. By the second day, she had stumbled upon a small shack.

Inside, she drank from a jar and found a tattered map pinned to the wall. El Refugio, marked with a small cross, was a place of refuge for those who had suffered at the hands of the cartel.

Hope flickered in her chest. She set off toward the town, encountering others along the way—some offering water and food, others warning of the cartel's reach. Yet with every step, her determination grew stronger.

El Refugio appeared in the distance, a ghost town in the shimmering heat. Martina approached, watching the signs of life—women tending to children, men repairing bullet-riddled walls. The people eyed her with caution, their faces hardened by years of suffering.

She recounted her story to Guillermo, the town's leader. His face darkened as she spoke of the cartel, his fists clenching in anger. "We will help you," he said. "But we must be careful. The cartel has eyes everywhere."

In the days following, the people of El Refugio tended to her wounds and shared their stories of survival. Martina felt a kinship with them—each one a testament to the strength of the human spirit in the face of unimaginable cruelty. But her focus never wavered. Joaquín was still out there, and she would not rest until she had him back.

As she gathered information, her path became clear. The rebels of El Refugio introduced her to a network of fighters, each with their own vendetta against the cartel. Together, they began to form a plan. They would infiltrate the cartel's stronghold, find Joaquín, and bring him home.

The journey to the rebel camp in the mountains was treacherous, but Martina pressed on, her newfound resolve burning brighter with each step. The rebels trained her, honing her skills in combat and survival. She learned to shoot, fight, and navigate the harsh terrain with deadly precision.

One night, as they sat around the fire, a young rebel named Carlos shared his story. Reyes had taken his sister, and Carlos had been searching for her ever since. His pain mirrored Martina's, fueling her determination even further. Reyes had to be stopped.

The day of the mission arrived. Dressed as a cartel recruit, Martina steeled herself for the task ahead. With the rebels' help, she would infiltrate the compound, rescue Joaquín, and make Reyes pay for the destruction he had wrought.

As she walked through the cartel's gates, her heart raced, but her expression remained cold. She had become the very thing she despised—an embodiment of the cartel's ruthlessness, all for the chance to save her son.

It was a dangerous mission, one that could easily cost her life, but Martina had come too far to turn back. The thought of Joaquín's frightened face and Emilio's final moments gave her the strength to continue.

As she lay in her makeshift bed, the mountain wind whistling through the camp, she whispered another prayer to the stars. "Guide me," she pleaded. "Give me the strength to save him."

At dawn, the rebels and Martina set out. They moved like shadows through the rugged terrain, each step bringing them closer to the cartel's fortress. The air was tense, the silence broken only by distant birds and the rustling wind. As they neared the compound, the stench of corruption grew stronger.

The plan was simple but risky: Martina would pose as a recruit, using her grief as cover to gain the cartel's trust. The rebels had given her the clothes of a fallen member, stained with blood and sweat. They had taught her the lingo, gestures, and the essence of the life she now had to embody.

The gates loomed before her, a symbol of the enemy's power. She took a deep breath, readying herself. The guards eyed her skeptically, but she kept her head down, mumbling rehearsed words of loyalty and vengeance. The ruse worked. They let her in, and she was swept into a world of chaos and brutality.

Inside, the cartel's regime was horrifying. Tortured souls, men and women alike, stared at her with vacant eyes, their spirits broken by the men she had hoped to save her son from. Martina focused on her son's safety. The stench of blood and fear clung to the air, and every exchange with cartel members required every ounce of her willpower to hide her true intentions. Her hands trembled whenever she glimpsed Joaquín's battered form, but she steeled herself, knowing one false move could cost them both their lives.

The rescue was painstakingly planned. At nightfall, the rebels would strike to create a distraction while Martina rescued Joaquín. The hours dragged on, each minute an eternity of fear and anticipation. She worked alongside the cartel members, her heart racing, her mind solely on her son's rescue.

Finally, night descended. Martina's pulse quickened as she saw the first signals from the rebels—flashes of light in the distance. The distraction came as planned. Explosions erupted on the perimeter, and chaos ensued. The compound was suddenly alive with shouts and gunfire, men scrambling to defend their stronghold.

Martina slipped away from her post, her heart pounding. Guillermo handed her a knife and a pistol. In the chaos, she slipped the knife into her waistband and the gun down her shirt. The compound was a labyrinth of shadows, each turn a potential dead end, her eyes scanning every shadow for danger.

She moved swiftly, her breath ragged. Her mind was sharp, focused on the task ahead. When she reached the area where her son and others were held, she saw two guards standing outside the door. She hesitated, her hand reaching for the knife. With a quick motion, she drew the blade, its edge gleaming.

The cold steel was a reminder of the brutal lessons from the rebels. She lunged forward, the blade slicing through the night. The first guard fell, a gasp escaping his lips. Chico, standing by the cage, was illuminated by flashes of gunfire. His gaze was fixed outside, unaware of the approaching danger.

As she neared Chico, she took a deep breath and struck. "Bastarda!" Martina called out. Chico, caught off guard, scrambled for his weapon, but Martina was faster. Her training with the rebels made her movements swift and efficient. The fight was fierce. Her knife cut through the air, narrowly missing as Chico fought back with frantic energy.

The clang of steel echoed through the alley, mingling with the sounds of battle. Chico swung wildly. Martina dodged, using her training to her advantage. With a sudden, well-placed strike, she cut across Chico's face from his right ear to his cheek, leaving a deep gash. He staggered back, clutching his wound.

Martina seized the moment, moving quickly to the cage. She grabbed the keys from Chico's belt and unlocked it, her hands trembling with adrenaline. Joaquín's eyes met hers, full of fear and hope. The door swung open, and there he was—bruised and battered, but alive.

She rushed to him, cutting through the ropes binding him. He collapsed into her arms, weak but breathing. Tears stung her eyes, but there was no time for relief. The battle outside grew louder, and she knew they had to move quickly. "Let's go," she whispered urgently, guiding Joaquín and the others out of the cage. Behind them, the sounds of battle grew louder, signaling time was running out.

Together, they stumbled through the corridors, the air thick with dust and gunpowder. They encountered other rebels, each offering a nod of respect and solidarity. Finally, they reached the exit. The battle raged on, a symphony of anguish and hope. Martina held her son tightly, her heart thumping. Freedom was within their grasp, but the cost was high.

The sight of Guillermo, bloodied but standing, brought a moment of relief. He nodded at her, his expression a silent question. She knew what he was asking. Reyes was cornered, his reign of terror ending. Her eyes searched the battlefield, and she knew what had to be done. For Emilio, Joaquín, and the village left in ruins, she would not stop until justice was served.

With fierce determination, she handed her son to Guillermo. "Take him to safety. I'll find you." Then, with a gun in her hand and a heart full of rage, she turned back, her eyes set on the man who had taken everything from her. Fueled by a mother's love, she faced Reyes.

Reyes was a formidable opponent, his cruelty evident in every move. Each step brought her closer to the truth she had to face. As she approached, she saw fear in his eyes, a fear she had never thought possible. Her rage grew with every beat of her heart, with every memory of her destroyed village and lost husband.

The room was a whirlwind of chaos. Martina's eyes locked onto Reyes. Her finger squeezed the trigger with calm resolve. The shot rang out, a note of defiance in the war. Reyes staggered back, a crimson bloom on his forehead. He looked at her, shocked, before crumpling to the ground.

The rebels cheered their victory. For Martina, it was bittersweet. The man who had taken her son and brought pain to her village lay lifeless. Her son was safe, but she had to ensure he never suffered again.

Guillermo emerged from the shadows, her son cradled in his arms. The boy's eyes searched hers, questions in his gaze. *Was it over? Was he safe?* With a nod, she assured him, and the weight of the world lifted from her shoulders. They had survived.

The night was a whirlwind as they retreated into the desert. The rebels had secured their victory, but at a high cost. As they made their way back to El Refugio, their losses heavy on their hearts, Martina felt a spark of hope. Her son was with her, and together, they would rebuild their lives.

The journey to the rebel camp was one of quiet reflection, the only sounds were the occasional sobs of the rescued villagers and the distant wails of the cartel's dying compound. When they reached the camp, older rebels were waiting full of relief and admiration. They had heard the news of the cartel's defeat, the stories of a woman who had stood against the swell of fear. The town had come alive in their absence.

In the days following, Martina became a symbol of resistance, a beacon of strength in a world losing its way. Her son grew stronger in her arms, the nightmares slowly fading into the comfort of her embrace. And as the village of El Refugio grew, she knew the love and resilience they had found here would be their salvation.

The story of the cartel's destruction was not the end, but the beginning of a new chapter. The fight for justice and peace was far from over, but with the rebels at her side and her son in her arms, Martina faced the future with the ferocity that had brought her this far. The scars of the past would never fade, but together, they would build a new life, as evidence of the power of hope in the face of unspeakable darkness.

Marisol, looking up from the fire, her voice gentle, "And you did, didn't you?"

Martina, smiling faintly, said, "Yes, I did. And now I see maybe all those struggles were leading me here, to this moment, with both of you."

Pilamar, glancing at Marisol, then back at Martina, "We've all faced our struggles. I've fought to protect Marisol, to keep her safe. But I find comfort in knowing we're not alone in this fight."

Martina, gazing into the fire, "Sometimes I wonder if all the pain and loss have any purpose. It's been so long since I lost my home, my husband..." Pilamar, quietly, almost hesitantly, "I understand more than you might think."

The trio stoked the fire and laid their heads down for the sleep they needed.

With Marisol tucked safely beside her, Pilamar lay awake, her thoughts racing. *The plan was simple but fraught with danger. They would slip away under the cover of darkness to conceal their escape. It had to be perfect. Any misstep would mean their capture and a fate worse than death.*

The fire burned down to a glow, casting a warm light on their huddled forms. As the night grew colder, they wrapped themselves in their blankets.

The days following their contact with the coyotes were a blur of sun-scorched afternoons and frigid nights. Martina had taught them more than just survival skills; she shared her strength, hope, and belief in a better life.

"Martina, I've heard about a secret tunnel running beneath the city. Those who know of its existence could use it to flee unnoticed. Do you know about this?"

"The tunnel is a labyrinth," Martina replied. "A damp, claustrophobic squeeze that seems to stretch on forever."

"Is it more dangerous than the way you cross?"

"It can be. It hasn't aged well. Parts may collapse without warning."

A distant rumble of thunder interrupted their conversation. Dark clouds gathered quickly, casting long shadows over the arid land. Without warning, the skies opened up, and heavy droplets began to fall, striking the earth with intensity.

Marisol was the first to react, eyes wide as the rain washed over her. She tilted her head back, letting the water stream down her face, rinsing away layers of dirt and exhaustion. Pilamar followed suit, stretching out her arms to embrace the storm, feeling the grime melt from her skin.

Martina stood still for a moment, her face turned to the sky, a rare smile breaking through her normally hardened features.

The rain fell in sheets, soaking them through, but they didn't care. For the first time in days, they felt clean—reborn under the power of nature. The dirt and despair clinging to their bodies slipped away, carried off in the streams running along the ground. For a few minutes, the rain was a gift, cleansing not only their skin but their spirits.

They packed up their camp and set off once more, their steps a little lighter, their hearts a little stronger. The journey ahead was fraught with danger, but they had each other, and that was more than any of them dared to hope for when they first set out. With every step, the image of sanctuary grew clearer in their minds.

As the sun reached its zenith, Martina called for a stop. They had reached the edge of the desert, where the landscape began to change. Martina pointed to a distant speck on the horizon. "Marisol, look," she said, her voice filled with excitement. "Eso es la frontera. That's the border."

Martina pointed to a section of the wall looking less formidable than the rest. "This is where we'll cross," she said. "It's not easy, but it's the safest way."

Pilamar swallowed hard, her eyes fixed on the towering barricade. "How do we get over it?" she asked, a mix of hope and fear in her voice.

"There's a ladder," Martina replied. "But it's a tight squeeze. We'll have to go one at a time, quickly. The patrols are less frequent here, but we can't afford to take any chances."

Marisol looked at her with wide eyes. "And if we're caught?"

"We won't be," Martina assured her, tightening her grip on the map. "We'll wait until nightfall. I'll go first. Once I'm over, I'll help you both up."

Pilamar's heart raced. Texas was so close she could almost taste it. But crossing the border would be the most dangerous part of their journey. They had to be careful, to stay vigilant. But with Martina by their side, they had a chance.

They approached the fence marking the end of Mexico and the beginning of the promised land. The metal bars stretched into the sky, a reminder of the world beyond their reach. The girl's eyes grew wide with wonder, and Pilamar felt a swell of pride. They had come so far and survived so much.

They waited until the moon had risen high, casting a silvery light over the desert. Then, with a deep breath, Pilamar took her daughter's hand, and together with Martina, they began to climb. The fence was tall and sharp, cutting their skin, but they didn't stop. They had come too far to turn back now.

As they reached the top, the sound of footsteps grew louder. They froze, their hearts hammering in their chests. A flashlight beam danced over the ground, searching for them. The Border Patrol was too close.

Marisol removed a sharp rock from her back pocket and flung it with all her might. The noise caused the guard to change his course. With a nod, Martina took the lead again. She had crossed this fence before and knew the way. They slid down the other side, landing in a crouch. The ground was hard, but the grass felt cool beneath their feet. They had made it. They were in Texas.

The three of them stood there, panting and bruised, staring at the vast expanse of land before them. It was a new beginning, filled with uncertainty and fear, but also with the promise of a better life. Pilamar took her daughter in her arms, feeling the warmth of her body, and whispered, "Te lo prometí. I promised you." She had given her daughter a name when she was born, a name carrying the weight of her dreams and aspirations—Marisol.

Marisol looked up at her mother, her eyes reflecting the moonlight. "Gracias, mamá," she murmured, clutching Pilamar's shirt tightly. "Thanks to you, we're here."

With a firm nod, Martina stepped forward. "Vamos," she said, her eyes gleaming with a newfound purpose. "I know a place where we can rest."

They followed her through the night, their footsteps muffled by the sandy soil and the stars above guiding them. After what felt like an eternity, they arrived at a small, well-kept house nestled in a hollow surrounded by tall grass. A sign swung lazily from a wooden post, reading "Mule-icious Lakeview Inn Bed and Breakfast."

"This is where I live," Martina said with a hint of pride. "It's not much, but it's safe."

Pilamar and Marisol exchanged glances. Safety was a luxury they hadn't known for a long time. They stepped inside, and the warmth embraced them like a mother's hug. The house was simple but clean, with the smell of herbs reminding Pilamar of her dear mother's kitchen.

As they sat around the table, sipping hot tea, Pilamar gripped her cup with both hands, her eyes clouded with old pain. "My husband, Mateo, was taken from me too, by the cartel."

Martina turned to face Pilamar. "I'm so sorry. What happened?"

Pilamar took a deep breath. "He was trying to stand up to them, to protect us. We had no choice but to confront them; they were threatening our family."

Marisol looked at Pilamar with concern. "Mama, it's okay. You don't have to talk about it if it's too hard."

Pilamar shook her head gently. "No, it's important. I need to share this. They took him away one night. We never saw him again. They left me and Marisol alone, vulnerable. I fought to survive, to keep my daughter safe. But it's the memories of that night that haunt me the most."

Marisol curled up on the couch as Pilamar recounted the events surrounding Mateo and the cartel. Martina listened, absorbed in the story.

Chapter III: Pilamar's Story

Mateo, Pilamar, and Marisol had just left La Cantina, their laughter echoing down the empty side street. The alley's shadowy jaws seemed to swallow the sounds of their footsteps.

Marisol shivered, clutching her Pap's arm tighter. "No me gusta cuando está tan tranquilo," she murmured. "I don't like it when it's so quiet."

Mateo chuckled, giving her a reassuring squeeze. "Relax, it's only an alley," he said, trying to sound more confident than he felt. In truth, he had heard about strange things happening around here after dark, but he wasn't about to let it ruin their night.

The alley was narrower than Pilamar remembered. Above them, flickering light cast erratic shadows across the cracked pavement, the only sound the distant wail of a siren. She stepped closer to Mateo, his presence a comfort against the encroaching alley walls.

Pilamar's heels clicked on the concrete, a rhythmic reminder of their progress. "You guys are dramatic," she said, trying to lighten the mood.

The figure in the shadows shifted, a glint of metal catching the weak light. It was a knife, the kind that left scars and told stories no one wanted to hear. Pilamar felt her stomach churn but forced herself to stand tall. This was their world now—a world where innocence was a luxury they couldn't afford.

"Dios mío! Pilamar..." Martina's voice faltered. "Please, continue if it helps you. Listening is all I can offer."

"Mateo was trying to stand up to the cartel," Pilamar continued, her voice trembling as she recounted the events of that night. "They had come for Marisol. They said she owed them something. We had no choice but to confront them."

The sound of shuffling footsteps grew louder, and the figure emerged from the darkness. It was a man, tall and broad, with a cruel smile that barely reached his cold, dead eyes.

"Chico, show them the price of crossing us," the man said, his voice a menacing growl.

Mateo nodded, his hand tightening around the object in his pocket. "I know," he said steadily. "But she's just a kid."

Chico took another step forward, the blade of his knife glinting as he flipped it open. "So was I, once," he said, his smile widening. "But my boss doesn't care about that."

Pilamar's heart raced as she watched the scene unfold. She knew Mateo had been hiding something from her, but she had never imagined it was this. The weight of his secret was a crushing burden, and she felt the walls of their precarious life closing in around them.

Marisol whimpered behind her, and Pilamar's resolve hardened. She couldn't let this monster touch her little girl. The air was thick with the promise of violence, the tension palpable.

"Let's talk," Mateo said, his hand still in his pocket. "There's got to be another way."

Chico sneered, his teeth gleaming in the dim light. "You think you can negotiate with us?"

Mateo's hand moved, and the man's eyes narrowed. In one swift motion, Mateo pulled out a gun, pointing it straight at Chico's chest. "I'm not asking," he said, his voice low and dangerous.

Pilamar's eyes widened. She had never seen Mateo like this before—so determined, so fierce. The other man in the alley paused, Chico's knife hovering in the air between them. For a moment, the world seemed to stand still.

"Back off," Mateo commanded. "Or I swear, I'll end this right here."

Chico took a step back, his smile fading. He knew when he was outmatched. With a nod, he slipped the knife back into his pocket and disappeared into the shadows, their footsteps fading into the night.

Mateo didn't move for what felt like an eternity, his gun still pointed at the spot where the man had been. Finally, he lowered his hand, his whole body shaking with adrenaline. He turned to Pilamar, his eyes haunted.

"You shouldn't have seen that," he murmured, his voice barely above a whisper.

Mateo's eyes closed as he took a deep, ragged breath. "They wanted to make an example of her," he said, his voice thick with pain. "To show us what happens when you don't pay your debts."

Marisol's whimpers grew louder, and Pilamar's anger surged. She had known the cartel was dangerous, but she had never imagined they would stoop so low. "We'll get out of here," she said firmly. "We'll leave tonight."

Mateo nodded, meeting her gaze. "We'll go anywhere," he said. "As long as it's far from here."

They gathered their things quickly, not daring to look back as they left the alley. The night was dark, but it felt lighter somehow, the weight of their decision propelling them forward. They had a long road ahead, filled with unknowns and dangers. But for the first time in a long time, Pilamar felt a glimmer of hope. They were together, and they were fighting back.

Days later, the quiet of Mateo's house was shattered by the sound of splintering wood. The door gave way with a resounding crack, and in burst the cartel members, their eyes hungry for the prize they had been denied. Pilamar's heart skipped a beat as she saw them, her fear for Marisol's safety more potent than ever.

"Where is she?" one of the men snarled.

Mateo stepped in front of Pilamar, his fists clenched. "Get out," he said, his voice low and menacing. "You won't touch her."

Chico from the alley smirked, his cruel eyes taking in the scene. "You think you can hide her forever?" he taunted. "You owe us, and we always collect."

The men grabbed the couple, pushing them to the floor. Pilamar struggled, her nails digging into the grimy concrete as she tried to break free. "Marisol, run!" she screamed, her voice raw with terror.

But it was too late. The little girl was already in their grasp, her small body trembling as they held her down. Chico took out a cigar, the acrid smell of it filling the room. He bent low, his smile widening as he brought the flaming end to Marisol's back.

"No!" Pilamar shrieked, her voice hoarse with pain as she watched the flame kiss her daughter's skin, leaving a trail of agony in its wake.

Marisol's screams filled the room, a sound that would haunt Pilamar for the rest of her life. Chico held the cigar there for what felt like an eternity, then pulled it away with a sickening hiss. The smell of burnt flesh mingled with the smoke, turning the air thick with the scent of fear and vengeance.

"If you won't come to our side," Chico said, his voice a cold whisper, "then she'll serve a purpose."

Mateo roared, his body straining against the men holding him down. "You'll never touch her again," he snarled, his eyes filled with a rage so deep it seemed to consume him.

Chico's smile grew colder. "We'll see," he said, his eyes lingering on Marisol's tear-stained face. "We'll see just how much you're willing to sacrifice to keep her from us."

As they disappeared into the night, the room remained still, the only evidence of their encounter the faint smell of fear and the distant echo of a promise made to a little girl with a scarred back and a doll with missing eyes.

Pilamar wept, cradling Marisol in her arms, her eyes fixed on the doorway where the monsters had disappeared into the night.

Mateo lay on the floor, battered and broken. "We have to go," he murmured. "We can't stay here, and the authorities refuse to help."

Pilamar nodded, her anger now a living, breathing force inside her. They had crossed a line, and there was no turning back. The time for hiding was over.

With renewed determination, they packed their few belongings, knowing they couldn't live in fear any longer.

Marisol clung to her mother, her small hand seeking comfort in the fabric of her dress. She looked up at Mateo with pleading eyes. He met her gaze, his own eyes full of sorrow.

They had managed to pack a few clothes and some food, but their escape was cut short. The screech of tires outside was their only warning before the cartel burst in. Chico stepped through the doorway, a cruel grin on his face. "Look what we have here," he jeered, eyes sweeping over the trio.

Mateo's arms were wrenched behind his back, handcuffs biting into his wrists. Pilamar's heart raced as she searched for an escape, but the cartel members had them surrounded, their grips on her and Marisol unyielding.

"You can't have her," Pilamar spat, her voice trembling with rage.

Chico leaned in, his breath foul from alcohol. "Oh, but we already have," he said, a gaze lingering on Marisol's scarred back. "And now, it seems we'll be taking the hero of the night as well."

With a rough shove, they propelled Mateo towards the waiting car, the engine purring like a beast. He didn't struggle, eyes locked on Pilamar and Marisol.

The car's tires squealed as it sped away, leaving Pilamar and Marisol in the dust. The night swallowed the taillights, taking with it the last of their hope.

Marisol's sobs grew louder, and Pilamar held her tighter, tears falling onto the girl's dress. "We'll get him back," she murmured, though she didn't know how.

Their escape attempt had failed, leaving them more trapped than ever. But Pilamar felt something else stirring inside her, something darker than fear. It was a burning rage, a need for vengeance that would not be quenched until every one of those monsters paid for what they had done to her family.

Martina, horrified by what she was hearing, was overwhelmed with sadness and grief for Pilamar and Marisol. "Is this why you gave everything you had to the coyote?"

"Yes. It was risky, but it was our only hope. We were leaving the hell the cartel had made of our home, hoping to start a new life in America."

"You need to rest," Martina advised. "Sleep while you can."

"You too. The morning will come quickly."

***

The sun shone through the cracks in the curtains waking Pilamar from her restful sleep. She changed clothes and washed her face feeling renewed and refreshed.

"Good morning, Martina. How did you sleep?" Pilamar asked, filling a mug with fresh coffee.

"Not well. I have things on my mind I need to share with you. Will you walk with me outside?"

"Sure. I hope it isn't anything bad."

"Well, that will be your call to make."

Martina revealed her dark secret. "This place," she began, her voice dropping to a whisper, "is more than just a sanctuary. It's where I get my revenge."

Pilamar's eyes widened. "Revenge?"

"Sí," Martina nodded solemnly. "I feed the coyotes and drug mules who come here, those preying on the desperate. But the food is laced with something... special. They don't make it across the lake or back to Mexico."

Pilamar's hand tightened around her mug. "What do you mean?"

"I poison them," Martina said, eyes hardening. "Then I take what they stole from others and sink their body there in the lake."

The revelation hung in the air, heavy and thick. Pilamar looked at the woman who had saved them, who had offered them shelter, and realized they shared a darkness. They were bound by more than just pain; they were united by a desire for justice.

The next morning, the sun painted the sky in pink and gold. The journey had forged a bond lasting a lifetime. As they walked, Pilamar felt a strange kinship with the coyotes roaming the desert, knowing not all of them were monsters. Some, like Martina, had hearts of gold and a fierce will to survive.

Days at the Mule-icious Lakeview Inn were filled with moments of quiet healing. Pilamar's bruises began to fade, and Marisol's laughter slowly returned. Martina taught them about the desert's secrets and the dangers lurking in the shadows. But it was her secret weighing heaviest on Pilamar's heart. Each night, she watched as Martina prepared food for the coyotes.

"Why do you do it?" Pilamar asked one evening, as they sat beside the lake.

"They're animals," Martina replied coldly. "They feed on the weak and the desperate. I give them what they want, and then take it back."

Pilamar nodded, understanding the bitterness fueling Martina's actions. She had seen firsthand the horrors some coyotes were capable of. Yet, she couldn't shake the feeling there was something more to Martina's vendetta.

"I will continue doing what I feel I must. You and Marisol can decide whether you will stay on and help...or leave me."

"I don't need to talk to Marisol, and I will not leave you on your own. Ever."

"You two can stay in the background, washing laundry and chores until you get a feel for how I deal with these bastards."

When the deed was done and the latest coyotes lay dead by the lake, Martina handed Pilamar a shovel. "We bury them deep," she said, "so they can't hurt anyone else."

They worked in silence, side by side. Pilamar felt an unexpected connection to the woman beside her—both had been shaped by tragedy, driven by the need for justice. The only sound was the distant call of an owl cutting through the night.

As dawn broke, they left the grim scene behind. The road ahead was long and fraught with danger, but they had each other. In the harsh desert, where the weak were often preyed upon, they had discovered their own kind of strength.

***

Years passed, and Marisol blossomed into a resilient young woman. Though the scars of their past had faded, they served as constant reminders of the arduous journey they had endured together. Pilamar dedicated herself to nurturing her daughter, and their bond deepened, forged in the fires of adversity. They had carved out a life for themselves at Mule-icious Lakeview Inn, a sanctuary amidst chaos.

One evening, a young coyote named Alejandro stumbled upon their haven. He was handsome, his smile igniting something within Pilamar that she hadn't felt in years. Yet it was Marisol who truly captivated him.

At sixteen, she exuded the maturity of a woman, tempered by the innocence of someone who had seen too much. Alejandro spoke of a better life in Mexico, where they could escape the relentless threats of La Migra, ICE, and border patrol. Marisol's eyes sparkled with hope as she hung onto his every word.

"Mamá," she whispered, "¿Podemos confiar en él? Can we trust him?"

Pilamar's gut tightened. She knew how easily desperation led people into danger. "Marisol," she said, her voice low and steady, "no te fies de su sonrisa. Don't trust his smile. These men are all the same."

Marisol searched her mother's face for reassurance. "But, Mamá, él no es como los demás. He's not like the others."

Pilamar took a breath, her mind flooded with the memories of horrors she'd witnessed. "You don't know what they're capable of," she warned. "They'll sell you, break you, and leave you for dead."

The tension between them grew thick. Marisol's eyes filled with tears, but she didn't look away from her mother's firm gaze. "Por favor, Mamá," she begged, "dame una oportunidad. Give me a chance."

Pilamar's heart battled between her love for her daughter and the painful memories of her past. "Fine," she said, "but if you're not back by dawn, I'll come looking for you."

Marisol nodded, determined. She understood the risks, but she knew she had to make her own choices.

As the night wore on, each minute felt like an eternity. Pilamar's mind swirled with fear and frustration. How could she have been so foolish to think they could escape the grip of the chulqueros/hustlers. In the desert, saviors and predators often looked the same.

When Marisol finally returned, her clothes were wrinkled and her eyes dark with fear. Pilamar knew immediately. Alejandro had tried to sell her, trading her safety for his own chance at a better life. But Marisol had fought back, her spirit just as fierce as her mother's.

"Where is he? Where's that bastarda?"

"I cut him with the slate shard and ran. I left him bleeding."

"Let's get inside," Pilamar said, rushing inside and locking the door behind them.

"Mama, I'm sorry."

"It's alright. Go wash your face and let me think."

Hearing the commotion Martina called out through the cracked door. "Pil, you sure you don't need me out there?"

Pilamar's voice was firm, yet laced with exhaustion. "We've got it under control. Marisol's tougher than she looks."

The mention of Marisol's name sent a shiver down Martina's spine. With a heavy sigh, Martina zipped her bag shut and as she approached the bar area she noticed Marisol's posture had changed, her usually vibrant eyes now clouded with a storm of anger and fear.

"What do you mean she's tougher than she looks? What happened?"

"She and Alejandro went for a walk and he brutally attacked her. She cut him with a shard she keeps in her pocket."

His viciousness was well-known throughout the region, a man whose cruelty was only surpassed by his cunning. Marisol had managed to defend herself with the sharp rock, a tool that had saved more than her pride.

Over time, the inn became a place where people could feel safe and find hope for a better future. But it was also a battleground, a stage for the silent war raging between those who sought to exploit. The three women knew Alejandro would not stand for this betrayal.

The sound of glass shattering and curses echoed through the corridors. The room quieted as the patrons hushed, sensing a deadly confrontation. Alejandro leaned against the counter, crimson lines marred his cheek and nose.

"Look who's back," he sneered, eyeing Martina up and down.

"I see you're happy to see me. It's written all over *your* face."

Pilamar tightened her grip on the baseball bat she kept under the counter. "Marisol's not your concern," she said, her voice a low growl.

The smirk on Alejandro's face widened. "She's everyone's concern when she's causing trouble," he replied, gesturing to his face.

Before he could say more, the door swung open. A figure filled the doorway, casting a long shadow across the floor. It was Alejandro's second-in-command, Carlos, his eyes wide with terror.

"Boss," he panted, "we've got...trouble."

Alejandro's smile faltered. "What is it?"

"It's...it's the border patrol," Carlos stuttered. "They've set up a new checkpoint. Right on our route."

The room held its breath. The tension shifted from personal vendetta to imminent danger. The game had changed, and the stakes were higher than ever.

"New checkpoint?" Alejandro snarled, pushing off the counter. "How did they find out?"

"I don't know," Carlos replied, his eyes darting around the room, searching for an escape. "But they're asking questions. They know something's up."

Pilamar's mind raced. The border patrol's timing couldn't be worse. With Alejandro on their doorstep, a raid could mean disaster for everyone.

"We need to move the goods," she said, her voice steady. "Now."

Alejandro's gaze flickered to the ceiling, then back to Pilamar. "Not without my cut."

"You're not getting a damn thing," Pilamar spat, raising the bat. "Not after what you did to Marisol."

Alejandro's smile turned feral, the light glinting off the gold tooth in his mouth. "You're in no position to negotiate."

Marisol stepped forward, the rock still clutched in her trembling hand. "I'll make sure you never lay a hand on anyone here again," she said, her voice shaking but resolute.

Pilamar nodded, her eyes never leaving Alejandro. "We don't have time for this. We need to get moving."

The room erupted into action. Martina grabbed her bag, adrenaline pumping. The smugglers scurried. Alejandro's eyes narrowed, calculating his next move.

"Fine," he said, a sly smile returning. "We'll settle this later. But for now, we work together."

The alliance was a temporary truce born of necessity. Collecting their contraband, they prepared to flee, the tension sharp. Alejandro's men glared at Martina and Pilamar, who exchanged wary glances. Their animosity simmered beneath the surface.

Once they hid the goods and warned the guests to leave, Pilamar turned to Alejandro. "Get out," she said, the bat still at the ready. "We'll deal with the patrol."

Alejandro studied her for a moment before nodding, his smile unwavering. "As you wish," he purred. "But remember, Pilamar. You owe me."

With that, he turned and strode out of the inn, his men following like shadows. The door slammed shut behind them. Pilamar, Marisol, and Martina stood in tense silence.

"We can't trust him," Marisol murmured, her hand still clutching the rock.

Pilamar nodded, jaw set. "But for now, we need to focus on the patrol. They can't find out what we're doing here."

The three of them moved to the window, peering into the dark night. The distant lights of the border checkpoint loomed closer with each passing moment. They had to act fast.

"You two stay here and keep the people calm," Pilamar said, her eyes hard. "I'll go deal with the patrol."

"But what if they recognize you?" Martina protested.

Pilamar gave her a grim look. "They won't. I've got a plan." With that, she disappeared into the night.

Martina and Marisol stood, wondering what her plan entailed. They had to trust her. For now, they could only wait and hope that the night would not bring an end to their operation—or worse, their lives.

Marisol took over the kitchen. She moved with swift precision as she served the patrons, acting as if everything was normal. Martina couldn't shake the feeling of foreboding that clung to her. She glanced at the clock, the ticking a relentless reminder of time slipping away.

Pilamar navigated the shadows toward the diner where her contact waited. She knew Alejandro would be too busy handling the checkpoint to notice her absence. At the diner, she found her contact, a wiry man named Jorge, already seated in a booth at the back. "You're cutting it close," he said, glancing around.

"I need the deed to the inn transferred to Alejandro's name. Now."

Jorge's eyebrows shot up. "Are you sure? That could put you in a—"

"Do it!" she insisted, urgency lacing her voice. "The border patrol is on us. I need him to take the fall."

With a resigned nod, Jorge slid the paperwork across the table. "Sign here. I'll handle the rest."

As Pilamar scribbled, a rush of adrenaline surged through her. This was her chance to turn the tables. With the deed transferred, she would make sure Alejandro's greed would be his undoing.

"Done," she said, shoving the papers back to Jorge. "You'll get the confirmation?"

"Tonight. Get back and be careful."

Pilamar hurried back to the inn, a fire igniting in her gut. She had a plan, and she was ready to set it into motion. The inn now belonged to Alejandro. The leader of the coyotes – smugglers who ruled the land with an iron fist was ill-equipped for this fight. But it was a small price to pay for what she had planned next.

Minutes stretched into hours, the tension thickening as the patrons' nerves grew taut. Every car that drove by, every flash of light sent a jolt of fear through the inn.

Then, the sound of an engine grew louder, headlights sweeping over the dusty parking lot. The women exchanged a look, hearts pounding in unison. Pilamar had returned.

The door swung open, and she strode in, her eyes gleaming with a mix of relief and triumph. "It's done," she said, voice low and steady. "The checkpoint's been...relocated."

The weight in the room lifted. "How?" Martina asked.

"Let's say I have friends in high places," Pilamar replied with a wink. "Or at least, friends who owed me a favor."

Marisol leaned against the bar, a hand on her chest. "So we're safe?"

"For now," Pilamar said, her smile fading. "But Alejandro won't forget this. And neither should we."

Their victory was bittersweet but a victory nonetheless. As the night wore on, the three of them cleaned up the mess Alejandro had left behind. Marisol reassured the scared migrants that they were free to continue their travels.

The Mule-icious Lakeview Inn bed and Breakfast became a beacon of hope in the desert. The name is a clever play-on-words. It obscured the malicious ends met by countless mules, coyotes, and smugglers.

They knew what they must do next. They had amassed a small fortune of the cartel's ill-gotten gains. They hid it beneath the floorboards—a treasure trove of gold coins, cash, and documents that could bring powerful men to their knees. Alejandro's operation grew more brazen by the day. It was only a matter of time before the cartel's wrath rained down on him. Now was their chance to strike back.

The plan was simple yet audacious. They would stage an accident—a fire that would engulf the inn, a tragic incident that could be pinned on the very men who had wrought destruction on so many. The bodies buried in the woods and sunk in the murky lake would surface, vilifying Alejandro as a monster. The townsfolk would believe that the gods themselves had turned against him, and the power he wielded would crumble.

Pilamar took a deep breath, the whiskey warming her blood as she turned to her companions. "We must be gone before the sun rises." Martina nodded, her eyes hard with determination.

Alejandro's men had taken her son, and she had sworn an oath to bring them down. Marisol, young and fiery, clenched her fists, eager for vengeance. They had suffered long enough under the coyote's thumb; now it was time to fight back.

They gathered the evidence of Alejandro's atrocities—the shackles that had bound their underage cargo, the bloodstained knives that had claimed so many lives. Each item served as proof of the cruelty that had infested their lives. As they placed them around the inn, the weight of their decision grew heavier. This was not about money or power; it was about justice, about reclaiming their humanity.

The flames started small, flickering at the base of the stairs. Pilamar frayed the lamp cord so the fire wouldn't spread too fast. They had to be gone before it became a raging inferno.

Martina's hand trembled as she watched the flames lick the walls. The wood crackled, and the acrid smell jolted her back to the night her house burned. Memories of the cartel kidnapping her son and the screams of her neighbors echoed in her mind.

Marisol noticed her friend's distress and grabbed her arm. "We have to go," she urged, her voice sharp with concern. "Now!" The smell of burning wood and the crackling flames grew louder. As the fire spread, they heard the distant wail of a siren, the fire department summoned by an anonymous tip.

Pilamar nodded. "We've done what we had to."

Together, they slipped into the night, the heat of the fire at their backs. The town was waking up, figures emerging from their homes to gawk at the destruction. They had set their trap, and now they could only wait for Alejandro to step into it.

They had played the coyotes' game, and now it was their turn to write the rules. The next morning, as the sun rose over the smoldering ruins, Alejandro returned to the inn, eyes full of greed. But as he approached, the sight that greeted him was one of chaos, not victory. The inn stood as a charred skeleton. His heart sank as the realization set in, cold fingers wrapping around his throat.

As he stepped closer, the clang of metal and murmurs grew clearer. Silhouettes of uniformed figures moved through the wreckage. The local police had arrived, along with investigators from the city. His eyes narrowed, mind racing to piece together what had happened. Had there been an accident? Or had someone finally turned on him? The thought sent a shiver down his spine. He took a step back, hand instinctively reaching for the gun at his side.

Police tape fluttered in the breeze. He tightened his grip on his weapon, resisting the urge to fight. He knew better; he would not fall to the authorities he had often evaded. With a snarl, Alejandro retreated into the shadows, mind racing. He had to find Pilamar, Martina, and Marisol. They had played him, and he would not rest until he had their heads on spikes as a warning to all who dared cross him.

The town buzzed with gossip and speculation. Some talked of the hidden sins of the inn's former owner. Others spoke in hushed tones of the bodies found in the lake and buried in the woods. Alejandro knew he had to act fast, before the noose tightened around his neck. He sent soldiers, those who understood the cost of failure, to track down the women who had outwitted him.

But the trail grew cold, and with each passing day, Alejandro's rage intensified. Town gossip turned to accusations. The eyes that once greeted him with fear now held suspicion. The fire had not only taken his wealth and power but also his reputation. He had become the hunted, a man with no place to hide. The coyotes had become the prey, and Alejandro vowed to make the hunters pay.

News of the inn's demise spread like wildfire, reaching the cartel's higher-ups. They had tolerated Alejandro's operations, but this would not go unpunished. The loss of the inn was a significant blow to their smuggling routes. The discovery of the bodies had drawn unwanted attention from the authorities.

Alejandro's position grew precarious as rumors spread. His pursuit of the trio took on new urgency, driven by the need to save face and appease his masters.

The three women vanished without a trace. Alejandro had to face the consequences of their actions. The coyotes' territory was no longer safe for him. He felt the hot breath of the cartel on his neck. Underestimating them was his undoing, but Alejandro was not going to stop hunting. As he plotted his next move, he knew the game was far from over. The flames of the inn had ignited a war.

Alejandro's men combed the countryside, turning over every rock. The trio remained elusive, their steps light and destination unknown. The cartel's anger grew with each passing day. The noose tightened around Alejandro's neck. The fire had not only taken his wealth but also his status. Without action, he would fade into a memory, thought of as a fool, and become a footnote in the cartel's history.

As the seasons turned the town began to rebuild. New faces appeared, eager to fill the void left by the missing trio. Alejandro watched from the shadows, mind racing with plans of retribution. He had to find them, not only to claim the fortune they had stolen but to restore his standing. They had bruised his ego and crippled him.

And so, the dance of predator and prey continued, each step measured and calculated. Alejandro's network stretched far and wide, but so too had the reputation of the trio who had brought him low. They had become legendary figures in the underworld. The game was no longer about survival; it had become personal.

Alejandro's reach was vast, but so too was their cunning. They had laid a trail of false leads and misinformation. No matter how hard he searched, he would always be one step behind. They had traveled over a thousand miles from the smoldering ruins of the inn. Using the cartel fund they bought land for a large building and a new home.

The project consumed them. Each brick laid, each coat of paint, and each wall built a fortress against the ghosts of their past. Drawn by their passion and determination the community embraced them with open arms. Becoming pillars of strength, they rebuilt lives shattered by violence and despair.

Martina's heart swelled as she listened to the stories of the women and children in the shelter. Marisol tempered her fiery spirit with the responsibilities of leading their new home. The thought of the cartel finding their way here never left their minds. They knew Alejandro would not rest until he had his vengeance.

Preparing for the storm they knew was coming they trained in the arts of self-defense. The skills that had once served them so well in their former lives turned their shelter into a fortress. They were no longer survivors; they were warriors.

The shelter stood tall and proud, and the women stood on the porch, watching the world outside. They understood the peace they had found was fragile, that the coyotes would come for them at some point.

But for now, they had each other, and they had a home. And as long as they were together, they would fight to protect it with every ounce of strength they had left. They knew the most powerful weapons of all were a deep lake and a backhoe.

###

Gritty Literature/Strong Female

*The spark for this story came from a play on words. I heard the word "malicious" said at one time, but I heard it as "mule-icious". That triggered a mental picture of drug mules and gang violence...the rest is history as they say...only in 6,800 words.

I did make the lead characters strong women because there needs to be better depictions of strong women.

No tripping over blades of grass while running for their life from a homicidal maniac.

That's been done to death—Hollywood!—come up with fresh stories and strong females, please.

The Frozen Smile of Lake Chautaugua

WINTERTIME IN THE SOUTH is rarely ever harsh. What little snowfall there is only lasts a few days before it melts.

The fresh snow is scooped from clean areas and made into snow cream.

The last serious winter storm was decades ago and was only ice that broke power lines and uprooted several trees.

In 2005, a great snow storm blanketed a small town in northern Mississippi. Kids amused themselves by running around throwing snowballs. People built their versions of Frosty the Snowman everywhere.

Little did they know that pollution in the atmosphere had tainted this snowfall. As the temperatures rose, the snowmen remained intact.

For weeks—snowmen made from the dirty and debris-filled snow dotted the landscape—eventual targets of BB gun-toting kids and rock chunking teens.

Yet, the snowmen remained intact.

There was a small tranquil lake in Tippah County that harbored a secret. Nobody knew for sure when the mysterious figure appeared on the water.

Even stranger—people were slow to realize the snowmen had disappeared—the water level of the lake had inexplicably risen. A cheery snowman figure made his home in the center of the lake, wearing a black silk hat and holding a shovel.

This snowman hid behind a nefarious smile as he knew what he had done.

Over time, he had been eating dry ice until he reached the sweet spot of remaining frozen. He then played the role of pied piper—luring the tainted snowmen to the lake—holding them under with his snow shovel until they had melted away.

To this day, he stands watch over the lake with the knowledge that he is still the only Frosty in this town.

*The spark for this story came from my cousin, Donna, who lives on a lake. She sent me a picture of a plastic snowman holding a snow shovel, leaning in the lake. She asked me to write a story about him. This is the original version I wrote for her. This sparked an idea for two more snowman stories.

The City of Speakeasies in the Galaxy of Prohibitionia

Act I: Trouble in the Blind Pig

Luna LaRue's galaxy of jazz and rebellion burned brighter than the twin suns of Prohibitionia. From her speakeasy—the legendary *Blind Pig*—she ruled nightlife with a sly grin and a voice like velvet soaked in moonshine. She was more than a lounge singer; she was the dame who made the underworld dance.

Tonight, the *Blind Pig* pulsed with life. Humans and aliens sipped smoky cocktails beneath chandeliers made from retrofitted reactor glass. Neon signs flickered like mood rings. The band played something that slinked through the air, and Luna's flappers—dames with killer smiles and *getaway sticks* sharp enough to slice steel—waltzed between tables, feathers flashing, weapons hidden in plain sight.

But trouble? Trouble never needed an invitation.

In the corner, three figures huddled over a greasy placemat. The *Cosmic Stooges*—Moe, Larry, and Curly—galactic-grade knuckleheads with a knack for chaos, were about to overreach.

"We hit her tonight," Moe barked, slamming his flask down hard enough to rattle the faux-chrome napkin holder.

Larry adjusted his twitching antennae and side-eyed a passing flapper. "Moe, those dames of hers? They ain't just dancers—they're trained killers. I heard one took out a bounty hunter with a rhinestone hairpin."

Curly scooped another bite of *Skyfin Salami Salad*, sighing dreamily. "Say what you will, this stuff's worth it. I ain't never tasted anything this smooth since the Grebulax barge buffet crash of '34."

Moe snorted. "You've got the Jake foot from eatin' too fast, not from contraband ginger, ya dope. One more bite and you'll be Jakin' with both legs."

Unbeknownst to them, Luna watched from behind the velvet curtain, her silhouette backlit in electric blue. She tapped her pearls—more comms device than jewelry—and whispered, "Stage left, three stooges, full of bad ideas and Skyfin." Her voice crackled into Glitter's earpiece, the lead flapper nodding from the bar as she poured a shot of asteroid whiskey for a drooling Torklaxian.

Luna stepped back. This wasn't her first rodeo. The game had already begun—and she always played to win.

Backstage, in a room scented with powder, perfume, and power, Wormy Willy squirmed under Luna's gaze. He looked like a heap of seaweed that had slithered into a zoot suit.

"You've been talkin', Wormy," she purred, circling him like a predator with perfect rhythm.

"Me? Nah, Luna—Miss LaRue," he corrected quickly, tentacles twitching. "Just makin' small talk in the Whisperin' Gardens, that's all."

"Small talk's fine. Unless it includes shipment routes, names, or *my* flapper schedules." Her smile glinted like a knife in a lamplight. "Spill."

Wormy wilted. "Okay, okay! There's a new crew sniffin' around—*The Comet's Trail*. Rumor is they're lookin' to carve up your slice of Prohibitionia."

"And the Stooges?"

"They're the distraction. The real play's coming from the east side. High rollers. One of 'em's got a red SE Cruiser with a cloaking upgrade—Name is Peter With the Pipes."

Luna raised an eyebrow. "Why should I care about some guy's jalopy?"

Wormy squawked. "'Cause nobody sees nothin'. He's got tinted panels, stealth mode, whole nine light years. He could drop you off at the docks and no one'd know it was you."

She leaned in, so close he could smell the whiskey on her breath. "You tryin' to help me get away, Wormy? Or are you plannin' your own exit route?"

Wormy gulped. "No, no! I'm loyal! Just sayin'... options."

Luna motioned to Glitter. "Keep him under wraps. He's got the *heebie-jeebies* and I don't trust anyone who jitters like a bomb with a bent timer."

Wormy tried to protest, but Glitter zapped him lightly with her glow stick baton. "Hush, you squishy snitch."

The stage lights dimmed. It was showtime. Luna pulled on her gloves, adjusted her pearls, and stepped through the curtain into a roar of applause.

Act II: The Flappers Strike Back

The *Blind Pig* was in full swing, its patrons sloshing cosmic cocktails and laughing like the world wasn't teetering on the edge of scandal and sabotage. On stage, Luna crooned into a chrome microphone, her voice velvet-smooth, slipping over the crowd like honey on heat.

Behind the velvet and neon, chaos was preparing to strike.

The Cosmic Stooges stumbled out of their corner booth, trying to look casual. They didn't.

Moe adjusted his collar and muttered, "Curly, hit the grid on my signal. Larry—doors. I'm going for the big cheese herself."

Curly patted the gizmo on his belt. "One zap and it's lights out, Moe. We'll be dancin' in the dark—nyuk, nyuk!"

Larry's antennae twitched like jittery tuning forks. "What if her flappers come at us? Last time, I saw one take down a bounty hunter with a stiletto and a wink. And the stiletto looked less painful."

Moe sneered. "They're dames in feathers. What're they gonna do—tickle us?"

Right on cue, Glitter strolled by in a swirl of sequins, flashing him a smile sharp enough to cut glass. Moe swallowed hard.

The Stooges slipped into position. Curly ducked behind a curtain. Larry sauntered toward the emergency exit, whistling off-key. "Don't mind me, just a regular guy with regular antennae… la-di-da…"

"On my mark… " Moe said.

The lights flickered—then died. Gasps filled the room. The speakeasy went dark, like somebody yanked the plug on the whole joint.

Backstage, flappers froze mid-costume change.

"Curly, you chowderhead!" Moe said.

Curly's voice yelped in the dark. "You said *on* the signal, woo-woo-woo!"

"My signal *was* the signal, ya numbskull!" Moe barked. "Move!"

But the flappers were already moving—sequins rustling like knives in the dark.

Feathers hit the floor as sleek weapons emerged. Glowsticks hummed to life in vibrant arcs of blue and violet. Chatter turned to battle cries. These dames had been trained for war in heels—and tonight, they meant business.

Patrons ducked as silhouettes collided in the shadows. Furniture splintered. Glasses shattered. The jazz cut off with a record scratch and was replaced with grunts, thuds, and a particularly pitiful whimper from Larry as he took a flapper's glowing rod to the knee.

Luna, unfazed, stalked toward the bar. She grabbed a bottle of star-aged whiskey and a flashlight, flicking it on with a snap. Her beam sliced the dark like a hot knife through cold cream.

"Looks like we've got uninvited guests," she purred into the mic. "Girls, let's give 'em a send-off they won't forget."

The lights stuttered back to life, revealing the Cosmic Stooges in a tangle of limbs, ropes, and feather boas. One of them moaned something about the *Jake walk*, only this time, he had it in both legs.

The crowd roared.

The flappers posed triumphantly, their glow rods raised high like victorious batons in a chorus line of vengeance. Glitter dragged Moe by the ear to the center of the floor and gave a bow.

Luna returned to center stage, flashlight still in hand. "Apologies for the intermission, folks," she said with a smirk. "Seems someone mistook us for amateurs."

A flapper tossed Luna a mic. She caught it with a flick of her wrist.

"The show will resume shortly. And drinks? On the house—for anyone still standing."

The band struck up again, rolling into a sultry number. The crowd whooped. The Stooges groaned. And the night's rhythm resumed as if sabotage had been just another verse in Luna LaRue's song.

Act III: The Dame and the Clipboard

The next evening, the speakeasy glowed like a jewel on the underbelly of Prohibitionia. Luna sat in her upstairs office, tallying receipts with one hand and sipping solar-aged rye with the other. The floor pulsed beneath her heels to the beat of jazz and jubilation.

Knock-knock.

She didn't even look up. "Come in, unless you're selling space insurance."

In walked a man who could sour milk just by standing near it—Mr. Jenkins, the planetary code enforcer, armed with a clipboard, a sour scowl, and the personality of a malfunctioning toaster.

"Miss LaRue," he said, eyes darting over the chrome fixtures and velvet trim like they were crimes. "We've had… complaints."

Luna raised a brow. "People complaining about being *too* entertained?"

"Structural violations," Jenkins snapped. "That stage of yours? Too springy. And you're missing a fourth emergency exit."

"Oh, we've got a fourth exit," Luna said sweetly, crossing her *getaway sticks* and leaning back. "It's just exclusive. VIP only."

Jenkins did not smile. "Interstellar liquor license?"

Luna gestured grandly. "Filed alphabetically in that cabinet labeled 'Mind Your Business.'"

The code enforcer scribbled something down like he was trying to break the pencil. "This establishment is in violation of at least thirteen statutes."

"You're in violation of ruining the mood," she replied, standing. "Care for a drink before you finish tanking my night?"

"No," he snapped. "What I care about is keeping this den of iniquity from collapsing onto its patrons."

"Well, you're in luck, Mr. Uptight." Her eyes gleamed. "We reinforced the floor after a flapper cracked it with her Charleston."

"It's *Jenkins*. And I'm placing these violations on file—"

He dropped a stack of paper thick enough to qualify as a blunt weapon. "Fix them, or I'll shut you down."

Luna watched him go, her smirk turning thin. She knew a storm when she smelled ozone.

She reached for her comm.

"Get me Stone," she said. "It's time we gave Mr. Jenkins something better to focus on than floorboards."

***

That night, the alley behind the *Blind Pig* glowed with the neon haze of promise and sin. Luna's heels clicked through puddles of spilled stars as she approached the figure leaning against the brick wall—fedora low, trench coat cinched, and a cigarette dangling from lips that had kissed more secrets than lovers.

"Detective Stone," she said, her voice soft as jazz smoke.

"Miss LaRue," he replied, tipping his hat. "What kinda trouble are we flirtin' with tonight?"

She handed him a slick silver data chip, its edges gleaming with secrets. "Jenkins. He's got a holier-than-thou attitude and a file cabinet full of violations. But guess what else he's got?"

Stone slid the chip into his pocket without looking. "Let me guess—moonshine, off-the-books credits, and a habit of frequenting establishments that *definitely* don't have four exits?"

Luna winked. "And a weakness for dancers who don't *just* dance."

Stone flicked his cigarette into the air like a punctuation mark. "Sounds like he needs a moral recalibration."

"I knew I could count on you," Luna said. "There's a bottle with your name on it at the bar. And Glitter's been practicing the shimmy just for you."

"For you, doll?" he purred. "Always a pleasure."

***

Within days, Jenkins was all but erased from Luna's path. Word spread fast—caught in a sting involving contraband ginger extract, two holographic twins from the outer moons, and a Jake walk that wouldn't quit.

The city's moral watchdog was now its punchline.

The *Blind Pig* thrived.

Luna? She sang sweeter than ever, her flappers twirled brighter, and not one soul asked about emergency exits again.

But behind the bar, Glitter poured drinks with one eye on the door.

Because in Luna LaRue's world, victory never lasted long—and the next problem always wore a new hat.

Act IV: Aether, Betrayal, and Stiletto Justice

The moonlight over Prohibitionia was thick with tension, hanging like jazz in a broken record loop. Inside the *Blind Pig*, Luna stood behind the bar polishing a glass, not because it needed it—but because her temper did.

Wormy Willy had gone missing.

Not in the "face-down in a speakeasy gutter" kind of way. No, this time, the slippery stool sample had taken off with something priceless: a vial of

Aether Lynx extract—the illegal, psychic-boosting serum harvested from a species banned in sixteen systems and whispered about in seventeen.

He was a one-cephalopod crime wave with a buttered eel's sense of loyalty.

Glitter tossed down her tray with a clatter. "He double-crossed us again, didn't he?"

"He sold us out for a fast buck and a getaway pod," Luna muttered, setting down the spotless glass. "He's making a deal with the *Skullcap Syndicate*—thinks they'll protect him once he hands over the vial."

"That stuff's worth more than a fleet cruiser," said another flapper. "We're toast if word gets out."

Luna's eyes narrowed. "We're not toast, sugar. We're the toaster. And Wormy's about to get burned."

***

The *Skullcap Syndicate* had taken up residence in an abandoned bathhouse near the power grids—a perfect spot for a quiet deal and a quick getaway. Luna and her flappers rolled up in style, dressed like dames at a dance-off and packing enough heat to fry a sun.

Glitter cracked her knuckles. "This feels like overkill."

"He's got the serum. That gives him teeth," Luna said. "We're here to yank them out."

They crept inside. Steam curled through shattered tile and moonlight pooled like mercury. At the center of the chamber, Wormy stood—slick and jittery—waving the vial like a showgirl's feather boa.

"I got what you asked for!" he whined. "Now where's my protection?"

A Skullcap thug stepped forward. "You'll get it once we test it."

That's when the lights dropped and the flappers struck.

From the shadows, sequins flashed like knives. Glow sticks cracked to life in a rainbow of violence. The Skullcaps never stood a chance. One caught

Glitter's heel to the forehead. Another went down choking on a mouthful of glitter dust and regret.

Wormy tried to bolt, but Luna was already behind him.

"You've got a real problem with loyalty, Willy," she said, grabbing the vial before he could twitch.

"It wasn't personal, Luna! It was business!"

She leaned in, her tone sugar and battery acid. "You made it personal when you crossed the line from coward to traitor."

She nodded. Two flappers grabbed him and dragged him toward the exit.

"Where to?" one asked.

"The alley. Let him *Jake walk* home with bruised pride and no memory of the last thirty minutes."

"How?"

Luna held up a small neural dampener. "Souvenir from the twins."

***

Back at the *Blind Pig*, the music swelled and the drinks flowed. Luna slid the reclaimed vial into her personal safe, next to a tiny silver locket and a plasma pistol with lipstick on the grip.

Another crisis handled. Another night survived.

But as the crowd danced and the jazz played on, Luna stood in the shadows behind the bar, scanning the room.

Wormy had sold her out for a taste of power. The Skullcaps had come for her territory. And the Aether Lynx serum? It wouldn't stay a secret forever.

She smiled faintly. The city could keep trying. But this dame? She'd outshine them all.

Act V: Radio Rebellion and the Last Call

The *Blind Pig* had weathered sabotage, betrayal, and one very flammable Skullcap scuffle—but what came next wasn't just trouble.

It was *Purity*.

The Interstellar Purity Corps—starched, pale, and powered by bureaucracy and bitterness—descended on Luna's district like a fleet of wet blankets. Their logo? A clenched white fist surrounded by a clean circle. Their motto? *Order, Silence, Obedience.*

It gave everyone the heebie-jeebies.

Luna sipped her coffee—black, no frills, just like her patience that morning—as Glitter read the bulletin aloud.

"Effective immediately: all venues promoting immoral entertainment must cease operations. Musical performances are hereby restricted to approved broadcasts. Alcohol distribution will be prosecuted as intergalactic misconduct."

Luna blew on her cup and murmured, "They came all this way to kill jazz."

"And sequins," Glitter added grimly.

The Corps didn't knock. They marched—straight into the *Blind Pig*, flashing warrants and sneers. At their head was Commander Blythe, a man so bland he made beige look like a primary color.

"You have violated seventeen purity statutes," he intoned, scanning Luna like she was a math problem he didn't want to solve. "Your establishment is hereby seized."

Luna didn't flinch. "You boys want a drink before you shut us down, or just a photo with me to hang over your sadness bunker?"

Blythe ignored her. "You are to vacate within the hour."

"Sure," she said, finishing her coffee. "Just let me grab my pearls and my *illegal soul.*"

They unplugged her microphone. Confiscated bottles. Smashed her backup saxophone—*the* saxophone that had once belonged to the jazz legend Lady Nebula.

But they missed one thing: the backroom radio station.

It wasn't much—just a dusty transmitter, a hot mic, and a hidden switch behind the absinthe barrel—but it was enough.

Luna LaRue went live.

***

"Good evening, beautiful souls of Prohibitionia," she purred into the mic. "This is Luna LaRue, broadcasting from somewhere *very* inconvenient."

Across the city, radios crackled to life. In apartments, alleyway hideouts, and hover-truck cabs, people leaned in.

"They shut down the *Blind Pig*. Said we were unfit. Too loud. Too colorful. Too *alive*."

Jazz slid beneath her voice like a slow storm.

"Well, I say forget silence. Forget the starch and the statutes. Turn up your dial and light up a bottle. Tonight, we're playing music they can't kill."

She clicked the switch. A trumpet wailed like a comet scream.

The flappers danced in the shadows. Patrons returned, guided by the pulse of outlaw sound. The Corps couldn't stop it—because it was already everywhere.

One of Luna's girls leaned in, breathless. "They're jamming our signal!"

"Let 'em try," Luna said. "We're broadcasting through six layers of reverb and two moon-bounced mirrors. If they catch us, I'll kiss their Commander on both cheeks—and sing at his retirement party."

Outside, a crowd gathered. Not just rebels, but regular folks. Shopkeepers. Welders. A granny who once tap-danced for smokes in '93.

They came to hear freedom. And Luna gave it to them.

One final set.

One final number.

She ended the night with a slow, soul-cutting rendition of *"The Dame Who Couldn't Be Silenced."*

And when the lights finally dimmed, and the mic cooled, and the Corps retreated—red-faced and legally outmaneuvered—Luna stepped into the empty room, heels clicking on the floorboards they never got around to condemning.

She looked at Glitter, who wiped her brow and laughed. "We just pulled off a full-scale radio rebellion."

Luna smiled. "And did it in heels, no less."

***

They say the *Blind Pig* never reopened.

That's not true.

It just went deeper.

Now it lives in whispers and music. In the clicks of hidden dials and the shimmer of sequins under street lamps. You don't find it—it finds *you*.

And if you're lucky, really lucky, you'll hear that voice again.

"Good evening, beautiful souls. This is Luna LaRue..."

###

Science Fiction/Humor

The Passage to Eternity

Part I: The Craftsman of Oak and Memory

Elwood Graves moved through his workshop with gentle precision, each motion deliberate, his face unreadable as the ticking clock on the wall.

His gnarled hands guided the chisel across seasoned oak, revealing soft whorls of grain beneath the blade.

Lacquer and sawdust smells filled the air — the perfume of his life's work. Every stroke honored the dead.

He had inherited his ancestors' skills—and their legacy of respect and awe. For generations, the Graves family had been known as artisans of the city's most exquisite coffins, each piece a tribute to the life it would cradle.

Though age had lined his face and silvered his hair, his hands still worked with the grace of ritual.

A faint creak from the door cut through the stillness. Light spilled into the room, scattering dust motes like tiny spirits in motion.

A young man stepped inside, hesitant but curious.

"Mr. Graves?" he asked, voice respectful.

Elwood didn't look up. "Aye." His voice was gravel over stone.

"I've heard of your reputation. I'd like to learn from the best—and I want to apprentice with you."

The chisel paused mid-stroke. Elwood lifted his gaze. The boy—no, young man—stood tall, eyes wide, hair combed back as if proving he belonged.

"You've got nerve walking in here like that," Elwood said, setting down his tool. "Most don't last the day. This isn't work for the faint of heart. It's long hours, and the company's mostly ghosts."

"I can handle that, sir."

Elwood's eyes narrowed, studying him. "What's your name?"

"Sam Thornton."

He nodded. "Well, Sam Thornton, we'll see if you've got more backbone than the rest." He extended a weathered hand. Sam grasped it, sealing the unwritten contract between them.

Under Elwood's watchful eye, the days grew into weeks. Sam's hands blistered, then calloused. His strokes grew steadier, his sense of reverence deeper.

Elwood spoke little, offering instruction in gruff fragments— "Measure twice," "Never rush the finish," "Respect the grain."

However, a rhythm existed between them, a silent understanding built from the smell of wood and wax.

One evening, as they polished an oak lid together, Sam asked, "Mr. Graves, why do you do this? Why dedicate your life to building these ... final homes?"

Elwood paused. The chisel in his hand hovered above the carving of a rose. His expression softened, the lines of his face shifting under the weight of memory.

"It's not just a job, boy," he said at last. "It's how I honor those who can't speak for themselves anymore." His voice dropped to a near whisper. "And it keeps their love within me, even after they're gone."

Sam followed his gaze to a small shelf in the corner. Upon it rested two carved figures—a smiling woman and a young boy, both rendered in careful detail, their eyes the same piercing gray as Elwood's.

"My Eleanor and Thomas," Elwood murmured. "She gave me a son who wanted to carve like me." His thumb brushed the wooden face. "But the fever took them both before his tenth birthday."

Silence hung heavy, the only sound being the faint crackle of the fire.

"I poured my grief into the work," Elwood continued. "Every coffin I build, I talk to them while I work. It's foolish, but it keeps them near."

Sam gulped, not sure what to say. "I'm sorry, sir."

Elwood gave a small nod, eyes glistening. "Loss teaches you more than life ever will. But it doesn't have to break you—if you let it shape you."

Sam nodded, the words settling deep.

Outside, night pressed against the windows.

Inside, the workshop glowed warm, oak mingling with the faint, comforting smell of coffee cooling on the stove. The silence between them no longer felt heavy—it felt like respect.

Part II: Apprenticeship and the Weight of Legacy

The months slipped through the cracks of the old workshop. Sam grew into his role under the steady rhythm of Elwood's instruction.

Every groove carved and lid fitted carried a ceremony—one that spoke of patience, precision, and respect.

Elwood didn't offer praise often, but when he did, it felt like sunlight in a dark place. "Good joinery," he'd murmur. Or, "That finish'll hold." Each word anchored Sam's resolve to learn not only the craft but also the reverence behind it.

When the day's work ended, Sam often lingered to sweep the shavings from the floor. Sometimes, Elwood would pour them each a small cup of coffee, the steam curling between them like the ghosts of words unspoken.

On one such evening, Elwood set down his plane and nodded toward the latest piece—a cherry wood coffin gleaming under the lamplight. "You've got a steady hand now," he said. "You're listening to the wood."

Sam smiled faintly. "I hear it creak and argue sometimes."

"That's it talking back," Elwood said. "Telling you where it wants to rest."

They shared a laugh before the stillness returned. Sam watched as Elwood's expression shifted, the humor fading into something deeper—an ache that had nothing to do with age.

"Do you ever stop missing them?" Sam asked, his voice careful.

Elwood's thumb rubbed over the wooden figures of Eleanor and Thomas. "No. But you learn to build around the emptiness. It becomes part of the design."

For a while they worked without words, the scrape of sandpaper and the rhythmic brush of varnish speaking for them both.

As winter deepened, the air grew sharp, and the light grew shorter. The townsfolk whispered about Elwood's coffins; they looked peaceful, as if the dead rested easy. Families came not only for craftsmanship, but for solace.

Sam noticed subtle patterns etched into the coffins—curving lines and symbols that looked older than any trade manual. "What do they mean?" he asked one afternoon, tracing a spiral with his finger.

"Bindings," Elwood said. "For protection. Tradition handed down through my family."

"Protection from what?"

"From being forgotten," Elwood replied. "Each mark tells the wood to remember the soul it carries. Forgetting is the worst death of all."

***

As the snow melted and spring crept in, their workbench filled with commissions. Each carried its own story, its own silence.

Sam's skill sharpened, but so did his questions. He felt the invisible pull behind Elwood's words—the way grief and craft wove together into something larger than either of them could name.

Late one evening, Elwood wiped his hands and turned to him. "Sam," he said, "you've got a pure heart. Don't let the world harden it."

"I won't, sir."

Elwood studied him for a long moment, then gave a slow nod. "Good. You'll need it for what comes next."

Part III: The Passage to Eternity

Spring ripened into summer, and the workshop settled into its rhythm again—the rasp of planes, the hum of saws, the heartbeat of the craft.

Sam worked beside Elwood as though they had been joined by an invisible thread. What began as an apprenticeship had grown into something closer to kinship.

One evening, as dusk bruised the horizon, Elwood rested his tools and gestured for Sam to do the same. "Sit a spell," he said. The lamplight haloed his silver hair, and for the first time, the older man looked both weary and content. "There's something I've never told you."

Sam pulled up a stool, curiosity bright in his eyes.

With his voice thick with reverence, Elwood began, "It's an ancient railway that carries the departed. The deceased and their kin embark on the final journey.

A magical train called the Passage to Eternity takes them to the Grand Cemetery, a place where the living don't tread. They say the rails were laid by angels and shadowed by devils," Elwood added. "Our family keeps the balance between the two."

Sam's brow furrowed. "A train? That carries souls?"

Elwood nodded, eyes distant. "Although the families return, they have no memory of the journey. It's as if crossing over wipes the slate clean.

The town cemetery is the only memory remaining. There they mourn and show respect. My family has long served as the guardians of that passage. Each coffin we craft must be worthy of that voyage."

Sam stared at him, unsure whether to smile or shiver. "You're serious."

"As serious as death," Elwood said softly. "It isn't about superstition. It's a duty. We ensure the balance between this world and the next stays unbroken."

A silence settled, deep and humming.

Elwood turned his gaze toward the corner where the wooden figures of Eleanor and Thomas stood. "When I lost them, I took them on the train. There's peace in sending your loved ones off in something you've made with your own hands."

"I can't imagine," Sam murmured.

Elwood's hand fell on his shoulder. "One day, you might not have to. You'll inherit this duty—if your heart remains as true as your craft."

Sam gulped. "That's a weighty thing to ask, sir."

"I know," Elwood said. "You needn't decide tonight."

The lamplight flickered as the wind blew through the eaves. The town bells tolled the hour, while the master and apprentice sat in thought, one sure, the other uncertain of faith.

***

With the seasons shifting, Elwood began a commission unlike anything prior. He spoke little, and when he did, his words came measured and strange.

Ancient symbols appeared across the oak panels—patterns Sam couldn't read but somehow felt pulsing beneath his fingertips.

"What are they this time?" Sam asked.

Elwood lifted his gaze from his task, weariness dimming his vision. "Bindings of passage. This coffin must serve not only the dead, but the realm itself."

The young man hesitated, unsure whether to press for more. The air in the workshop felt charged, as though a storm hovered beyond the walls.

That night, after Sam had gone home, Elwood worked by the low flame of an oil lamp. His calloused hands traced the last carved line into the wood, the strokes deliberate, reverent. The clock ticked behind him, its pendulum marking the breath between worlds.

The tension between master and apprentice grew in small, imperceptible ways. Sam's skill had bloomed—too hastily, perhaps—and admiration blurred into ambition.

He wanted to craft coffins as fine as Elwood's, to have townsfolk whisper his name with the same reverence.

How does he carry death with such peace? Sam wondered. *If I could build as he does, I'd feel that peace too.*

One evening, Rachel invited Elwood to supper. The smell of roasted chicken and thyme filled the modest home, and laughter from the children spilled through the doorway.

Elwood felt like family again.

Rachel set a plate before him. "You work him heavy, Mr. Graves," she said with a gentle smile.

"He's worth the work," Elwood replied. "Has a gift in his hands."

Sam chuckled but didn't look up. "A gift I plan to improve."

Rachel's gaze lingered on her husband. "You look at your work like it's the only world that matters, Sam. Don't forget who's still breathing beside you."

Elwood's brow furrowed, but he said nothing. He raised his glass. "Salute to improvement—and the wisdom to guide it."

Rachel caught the shift in tone, her smile fading. When the meal ended, she pushed back her chair, then leaned forward on her elbows, eyes fixed on Elwood. "You've both been at this so long—don't you ever tire of death as company?"

Elwood's fork paused midair. "Death isn't the company," he breathed. "It's a reminder to live right."

Later that night, as Rachel tucked the children into bed, Sam returned to the workshop. The coffin Elwood had been building glowed under lamplight, its carvings intricate, its panels marked with symbols that hummed when he neared.

Bindings of passage, Elwood had called them.

"But meaning changes nothing. Every craftsman must guard his heart as carefully as his work."

The older man reached for the coffin's edge and slid the lid shut. The click echoed like a last prayer. But as Sam traced one with his finger, the lines shimmered, rearranging beneath his touch. The lamplight flickered, though no draft stirred. The tools on the wall trembled, and the wood itself appeared to take a breath.

"What are you doing, boy?" Elwood's voice filled the doorway.

"I wanted to understand," Sam stammered. "You keep secrets—teach me everything, or I'll never be more than your shadow."

Elwood's eyes hardened. "Some things aren't meant for mortal hands. You tamper with them, and they'll answer."

The lamp flickered.

The air grew cold.

A thin ribbon of black smoke seeped from the coffin's seams. It twisted upward, coalescing into a shape that pulsed like a dying ember. Two red eyes flared to life.

"You," Elwood whispered. "You shouldn't exist."

The specter's laughter slithered through the room. "Oh, I exist because of you, coffin-maker. Every bond your line has forged became my prison."

Elwood's pulse quickened. "You seek to destroy the Passage—to unbind the dead?"

"To end it forever," the specter hissed. "Let the worlds merge and chaos reign."

The workshop trembled. The unfinished coffin rattled, its carvings glowing like embers.

Elwood seized a chisel and drew a quick circle of salt around the coffin. "Get back, Sam!"

The specter's tendrils lashed outward, knocking tools from the bench. "Your craft binds me no longer," it thundered. "The boy's pride has cracked your spell."

Elwood chanted—low, ancient words inherited through blood and grief. The specter reeled, but the strain etched pain into Elwood's face.

Sam, frozen near the wall, saw the man he had envied now trembling under the weight of generations. "Mr. Graves!" he shouted.

Elwood's voice broke. "Hold faith, Sam—believe in the craft, not the glory!"

The specter surged, striking the lamp. Flames whooshed to life, licking the floorboards.

In desperation, Elwood thrust his hands onto the coffin lid, pressing his palms against the glowing runes.

The light flared.

Its form tearing apart, the specter screamed as it was drawn back into the bindings.

The fire died.

The silence returned, deep and absolute.

Elwood sank to his knees, his breathing ragged. The carvings dimmed to faint warmth.

Sam stepped forward, guilt, and awe warring on his face. "I didn't mean—

"I know," Elwood grasped the coffin's edge and slid the lid shut. The click echoed like a last prayer.

Outside, the night surrendered to dawn. The air smelled of rain and fresh earth.

Elwood whispered, "May it hold."

Part IV: Balance in the Necropolis

The morning of departure dawned pale and cold. A thick mist clung to the streets, curling around the lampposts like restless fingers.

Elwood guided the horse-drawn carriage toward the station, the currently empty coffin secured in back beneath a heavy black cloth.

At the depot, the platform stood empty except for a single iron train—its paint a deep obsidian, its trim veined with silver that shimmered even in the weak light.

Elwood climbed aboard and took a seat near the coffin car. The door hissed closed behind him, sealing him in with silence.

The train lurched forward.

The steam—created by the wood burning furnace hissed—wheels clattered against rails that glowed in an ethereal blue.

Outside, the scenery shifted—from the gray stone of the city to vast fields bathed in unimaginable light.

Colors pulsed and changed like liquid glass.

Elwood bowed his head. *Guide them safely. Let the passage hold.*

Apparitions appeared one by one along the rows—familiar faces blurred by memory, their eyes distant yet kind. They said nothing, but their presence filled the car with warmth.

A tremor shook the floor.

The lights flickered.

Then came the whisper—low and scraping, threading through the metal walls like wind through a graveyard gate.

From the far end of the car, a figure emerged—a grotesque silhouette wreathed in shadow and smoke—radiating malice and decay.

Its eyes glowed crimson, and its mouth stretched into something that might once have been a smile.

Elwood rose. "You're not welcome here."

The specter laughed, a hollow, shuddering sound that made the windows rattle. "You bind what should be free," it hissed. "Your line of builders keeps us chained."

Elwood's heart thudded, but his voice stayed steady. "Our duty keeps balance. You seek chaos."

The specter lunged, its form rippling like smoke in the wind. Elwood thrust out a trembling hand. The carvings on the coffin flared to life, their symbols burning white.

The air crackled with unseen energy.

Elwood staggered forward, chanting words older than memory—syllables that tasted of earth and fire. "Ligare hoc malum, bind this evil."

The specter howled as the light drew it backward, its form unraveling in threads of black mist.

"Aequilibrium inter bonum et malum serva, maintain the balance between good and evil!"

The coffin's lid lifted, glowing from within. The specter—a former necropolis guardian—shrieked, twisting as the ancient magic pulled it inward, binding it tight.

With a last cry, it vanished into the waiting dark.

The train stilled.

The lights steadied.

One by one, the apparitions faded from sight, leaving only the faint scent of lilac and smoke.

Elwood sank into his seat, chest heaving. His palms glowed with the same light that sealed the coffin. "Rest now," he whispered.

The conductor, his eyes filled with gratitude, approached Elwood and clasped his hand. "You've done a great service. The afterlife can never repay the debt," he said.

Elwood managed a nod. His chest heaving he knew his task was not finished. He still had to lay the soul to rest and complete the ritual.

Outside, the horizon started birthing dawn—a pale, forgiving gold.

In the necropolis, gravestone cast long shadows, and the air was perfumed with lilies and fresh-turned earth. Elwood felt the watchful gazes of spirits as he guided the procession along the path.

Arriving at the burial site Elwood prepared for the final act.

As the coffin was lowered into the earth the ground trembled. Elwood took a deep breath.

Each movement was deliberate, and as the last bit of dirt covered the grave, a sigh of relief exhaled from the necropolis.

Part V: The Burden Shared

For days, the workshop sat silent. The air still smelled faintly of smoke and sanctity. Sam swept the ashes, oiled the hinges, and polished the coffin to a soft gleam.

When he turned, he found the older man sitting near the window, pale but alive, hands bandaged, eyes distant.

"You should've let me face it," Sam whispered.

Elwood gave a tired smile. "You weren't ready. But one day you will be."

He gestured toward the coffin. "That's not just oak and iron. It's a seal. What we build holds the world together, Sam. Every nail, every carving—it's a promise."

Sam nodded, his throat tight. "I nearly broke it."

"And you learned why we don't chase greatness for ourselves." Elwood's gaze softened. "The craft's meant to serve, not shine."

Outside, a slow drizzle fell, dappling the windowpane.

Rachel entered the workshop, worry etched on her face. "You both look like you've been through hell," she said, kneeling beside Elwood.

He gave a low chuckle. "In a manner of speaking."

Sam watched her take his hand. "You were right," he said. "Death isn't our company—it's our reminder."

Elwood nodded. "Aye. Remembrance embodies true living."

***

Weeks later, Elwood's health waned. The toll of the binding had drained him more than he admitted.

One morning, Sam found him at the workbench, with a faint smile resting on his lips, the chisel still in his hand.

The faint light from the window bathed him in gold.

Sam knew what to do.

He prepared the wood himself— dedicated—every curve carved with gratitude and grief. The inscription—*Christi vobiscum, Go with God*—he carved with love.

The last coffin Elwood Graves would ever occupy shone with perfection.

When the townspeople gathered to pay their respects, they spoke of the master artisan who had built peace into every seam.

Sam stood apart, his face calm but his eyes glistening with tears.

After the ceremony, he returned to the workshop.

The tools still waited—arranged with Elwood's precision—the chisel waited silent, but ready.

The small wooden figures of Eleanor and Thomas stood by the window, catching the morning sun.

Sam set his hands on the bench and whispered, "I'll keep it, sir—the promise, the passage, all of it."

The air shifted.

For an instant, he could've sworn he heard the low wail of a train whistle fading into the distance.

He smiled. "Safe travels."

Outside, the mist rolled across the hills, catching the first light of day.

And somewhere beyond the veil, a train thundered on—its rhythm eternal, its promise unbroken.

###

Supernatural/Speculative Fiction

The Snowmen of Tippah County

The ice storm of '94 came out of nowhere, coating Tippah County in a brittle, gleaming armor. Trees bent and cracked under the weight, and the roads turned into a treacherous maze of frozen glass.

A week later, as if the storm hadn't done enough damage, snow fell. At first it was beautiful — soft flakes drifting down like feathers from heaven. But the beauty was only a disguise.

Tammy, Tina, Sean, and Todd, four kids with more bravery than sense, built sleds and flew down icy hills, their laughter ringing through the cold. It was a winter the town had never seen before.

From her office window, Mayor Hazel — known to her childhood friends as Duddy — watched the children play. *I've lived here my whole life,* she thought, *and heavy snow never comes without trouble.* She grabbed her coat and stepped out into the frozen world.

The town square filled quickly with families shaping snowmen. Carrot noses, coal eyes, scarves, and hats — it was a scene from a Christmas card. Then, the children noticed something strange.

The eyes of every snowman glistened with an eerie light, and their smiles widened, sharper, crueler, with each passing flake.

The first attack came without warning. A snowman reached out with a crackling arm and grabbed a boy's scarf, yanking him close. The child's mother screamed, frozen in place, until Mayor Duddy tore the child free. The snowman tilted its head, almost curious, before lunging again.

"Inside! Everyone inside!" Duddy shouted, dodging the icy swing.

Panic swept through Tippah as snowmen across town moved, their jerky motions growing smoother, their eyes burning with a cold, unnatural fire.

Tammy, Tina, Sean, and Todd huddled together, determination replacing their laughter. Sean repeated a half-remembered tale about Dumas Lake.

"The water there's strange. If we melt them, maybe it'll stop."

Buckets were filled, sleds loaded, and the four children — with Mayor Duddy at their side — marched back to the square. Water splashed against the snowmen, hissing as the creatures screamed and withered into slush.

Townsfolk cheered and joined the fight, but for every snowman that fell, more rose.

Snow wasn't falling — it was breeding.

The bakery owner dashed out with sacks of baking soda to neutralize the acid. Farmers brought feed troughs to carry more lake water. Tippah became a war zone of fire, water, and ice.

But the snowmen were clever; they began hurling ice shards, cutting through the barricades and windows alike.

"We can't hold them forever," Mayor Duddy cried.

Tammy had an idea. "If lake water weakens them... what if we bring the whole lake?"

It was reckless and desperate — but it was all they had. Together they trudged through waist-deep snow to Dumas Lake. The black ice groaned beneath their axes until, with a shattering crack, the water broke free. A torrent rushed toward Tippah, flooding the square just as the sun broke the horizon.

The townsfolk watched in awe as the snowmen shrieked, their bodies hissing, steaming, and collapsing into puddles of dirty slush. Relief swept over Tippah, though the buildings stood scarred and the people shaken.

In the days that followed, neighbors helped neighbors, rebuilding stronger than before. But whispers spread. Some swore a meteor had poisoned the snow. Others muttered about curses older than the county itself.

Years passed. The children grew up, each carrying the memory of that winter. Every December they gathered at Dumas Lake, tossing a handful of fresh snow into the water as tribute.

Tourists came, eager for the tale of the children who fought living snowmen. Some claimed they saw ghostly figures in the fog, snowmen's eyes glowing faint in the tree line.

And every winter, as the first flakes fell, Mayor Duddy — older now, but sharp as ever — would look out her window and smile, just a little. She knew Tippah was ready for whatever storm might come.

But deep in the forest, when the wind was just right, two glowing eyes sometimes stared back.

The town had grown cautious but not fearful, prepared for the unexpected. Sean, now the town's sheriff, kept a close watch on the weather reports, his mind never at ease.

Tammy had become the local schoolteacher, imparting knowledge to the new generation. She told the story of the snowmen in her lessons on the importance of teamwork.

Tina, the town's doctor, had treated the injuries that day and had since dedicated her life to healing the town.

Todd, a skilled engineer, had used his knowledge to design a system that floods the town with water from the lake in case of another attack.

Mayor Duddy had retired, leaving the town in the capable hands of a council that she had mentored. Her legacy of courage and leadership lived on in every corner of Tippah.

Speculative Fiction

*The spark for this story, and for 'The Alchemist's Folly' came to me a few years back. My cousin lives on a lake in Tippah County, she asked me to write a story about the plastic Christmas snowman holding a bright orange, or faded red, snow shovel decoration that appeared in the lake.

Nobody knew the—who?, why?, when?, or how?—so I jotted down something and sent it back. But, my mind wasn't happy with that, so I wrote a couple more about snowmen, until I guess I purged it from my system.

**Okay. My explaining how the spark for this story came about made me think about that original snowman story request. I went onto Facebook and copied the story, and I'll add it to the list.

The Boy and the Sands of Al-Khayal

IN THE BUSTLING HEART of a desert town, a solitary figure emerged from the shadows of a narrow alley. The sun blazed overhead, casting sharp lines across the dusty streets, and the air carried the scent of spices and the murmur of distant motors.

This man, tall and stooped, with a weather-beaten face and eyes the color of shifting sands, was known only as Al-Khayal.

His days were spent in quiet contemplation, his nights in pursuit of an elusive trade. His gait was deliberate, a soft shuffle that barely disturbed the sands beneath his worn leather sandals.

The fabric of his thobe billowed gently around his lean frame, whispering secrets to the wind that carried them away into the vast, uncaring expanse of the desert.

Al-Khayal approached a ramshackle stall where a young boy sat cross-legged, surrounded by a jumble of wooden toys. The boy looked up, his eyes wide with curiosity as the stranger's shadow fell over him.

His skin was dark from hours of play under the unforgiving sun, and his smile was as bright as the gleaming dunes stretching to the horizon.

"As-salaam 'alaykum, *Peace be upon you*" Al-Khayal greeted, his voice a gentle rasp that seemed to hold the whispers of ancient tales.

The child nodded shyly, his hands resting on a miniature camel carved with surprising skill. "Wa 'alaykum as-salaam, *And peace be upon you*," he replied, his voice like the tinkle of distant bells.

Al-Khayal studied the toy for a moment, his eyes lingering on the intricate patterns etched into the wood. "Your work is as fine as the grains of sand," he said, his gaze steady. "But they are not toys that I seek today." He leaned closer, his voice dropping to a near-whisper. "I am in need of something... special."

The boy's curiosity grew, and he leaned in, his smile fading to a look of solemn understanding. He whispered a few words into the man's ear, and Al-Khayal's eyes lit with a knowing spark. He reached into the pocket of his thobe and pulled out a handful of coins, placing them in the boy's small, outstretched hand.

The child's eyes widened at the silver glinting in the harsh light.

"Meet me at the edge of the desert tonight," Al-Khayal instructed, his voice low and urgent. "Bring what I need."

With that, he turned and disappeared into the swirl of fabric and heat that was the marketplace, leaving the boy with his thoughts and his newfound treasure.

The sun continued to beat down on the toys, casting them in a warm, golden light, but the boy's mind was already racing with the promise of adventure that lay beyond the dunes.

He had no idea that the sand he played in was a commodity more precious than gold in the hands of those who knew its true worth.

**

As the sun sank, the boy packed up his stall and set off for the desert's edge. His heart raced with excitement and a hint of trepidation as he approached the meeting place, a spot where the town's lights grew faint and the desert's vastness swallowed the horizon.

When Al-Khayal appeared, the boy was already there, scanning the horizon for any sign of the elusive sand that had brought the mysterious man to his doorstep.

The man's silhouette grew larger as he approached, and with him came the scent of exotic spices and the promise of something extraordinary.

"You have it?" Al-Khayal asked, his voice a blend of urgency and anticipation.

The boy nodded, reaching into the folds of his own thobe to produce a small leather pouch. He held it out to the man, whose long, slender fingers closed around it with quiet precision.

The pouch felt heavy, and the boy could almost hear the grains of sand shifting inside.

Al-Khayal opened it, letting a trickle spill into his palm.

The sand shimmered in the moonlight, each grain catching the faint glow of the stars above.

The man's eyes narrowed as he examined the sand, his expression unreadable. "This is good," he finally said, his voice a low rumble of satisfaction. "Very good."

The boy felt a surge of pride. He had never known the significance of the sand that sometimes found its way into his toys, but now, holding this pouch, he realized he had been a custodian of something far greater than playthings.

The boy frowned. "Why do they want this sand so much? We're surrounded by it."

Al-Khayal closed the pouch and slipped it into his robes. "Your father was a wise man," he said, his eyes lingering on the boy. "He understood the value of what lies beneath our feet."

The boy nodded solemnly, feeling the weight of his father's legacy settle on his shoulders. "What will you do with it?" he asked, his curiosity getting the better of him.

Al-Khayal knelt beside him, his expression somber. "Not all sand is the same," he explained, sifting the grains between his fingers. "The desert's sands have been shaped by the wind, their grains too smooth to bind together—useless for building. But this..."

He removed a pinch of the maritime sand, its rough edges catching the light. "This sand has traveled from the ocean's depths. It holds the strength to build towers, cities, and empires. Without it, progress halts."

The boy's eyes widened as the weight of the truth settled on him. His father's words echoed in his mind: *Guard the sands, for they guard us.* Yet he could not ignore the sadness in Al-Khayal's voice. "So they take it from us?"

Al-Khayal smiled, a rare sight that softened the harsh lines of his face. "With this," he said, holding up the pouch, "You and I will build a future for many."

The boy looked out at the desert, the endless sea of sand stretching before him, and for the first time, he saw not just a playground but a world of possibility.

The wind whipped at their clothes, carrying with it the whispers of ancient trade routes and the dreams of those who sought to conquer the sands.

Al-Khayal nodded, his expression grim. "Countries covered in sand buy this from us because their own deserts betray them. And if we let them strip it all away, the price will not just be theirs to pay."

As they turned toward the heart of the desert, a sound broke the stillness—faint, yet distinct. The boy froze, his breath caught in his throat.

Al-Khayal motioned for silence, his eyes scanning the horizon.

A distant figure appeared, silhouetted against the starlit dunes.

Then another.

"Traitors," Al-Khayal hissed under his breath. "They would strip the land bare for coins."

The boy's pulse quickened. "What do we do?"

Al-Khayal tightened his grip on the pouch. "We protect what is ours," he said firmly. "The sands have endured centuries of storms. They will endure this, too."

***

The figures drew nearer until the boy could see the glint of metal beneath their cloaks. Al-Khayal pressed the pouch into his hands. "Go," he whispered. "Let the desert remember us kindly."

Before the boy could protest, the man strode toward the approaching shadows. A gust of wind rose from the dunes, swirling the sand into a golden veil that swallowed everything in its path.

When the storm settled, Al-Khayal was gone, the traitors vanished, and the desert lay unbroken once more.

The boy stood alone—behind him, the dunes shifted as if breathing, and he realized the sands had chosen their guardian.

He turned toward the horizon, where dawn was beginning to smudge the stars, and whispered the words his father once told him—*Guard the sands, for they guard us.*

Then he walked on, his footprints fading with the wind.

###

Literary Fable / Environmental Allegory

*The spark for this story is a second version after seeing a bit of trivia that Australia sells their sand to other countries to use as building material because the country's own sand is too inferior.

Dorian, the Ink Drinker

IN THE QUIET UNIVERSITY town of Elmswood, the chime of the library's grand clock echoed across cobblestone streets. The air smelled of paper and ink.

Dorian Ravenscroft, a scholar of sharp intellect and sharper ego, was a fixture among the faculty. His townhouse stood between the University quadrangle and the winding road leading to the city.

Inside, his library—half study, half sanctuary—was lined floor to ceiling with books, the shelves sagging beneath their weight. Dust drifted through lamplight like tiny ghosts of the past.

Rachel and Michael, his closest friends, were frequent guests. Rachel, a literature professor with a gift for drawing others out, paired easily with Michael, a genial historian known for his humor and calm.

Their gatherings always took place in Dorian's library, where decanters and conversation flowed freely.

One evening, as the scent of port and candle wax mingled, something shifted. The trio was deep in debate over an alchemical manuscript when a soft thud interrupted them.

A book—one Dorian swore had never been there before—rested on the far table. Its cover was dark leather, edges mottled with age, its yellowed pages visible through a split binding.

"What's this?" Dorian murmured, crossing the room. He brushed away the dust; the title was long gone. When he opened it, the scent of iron and parchment rose like breath from a tomb. The handwriting was elegant, slanted, unmistakably personal. "It appears to be a diary," he said.

Rachel laughed. "Maybe one of your ghosts finally returned an overdue book."

Michael frowned. "That wasn't there before dinner?"

"No," Dorian said, eyes fixed on the ink. "It wasn't."

When the others left, Dorian lingered. Candlelight flickered across his face as he pored over the strange volume. It spoke of scribes who sought to consume knowledge itself—ink distilled from words, enlightenment through ingestion. Each page deepened his fascination.

Its words offered knowledge beyond reach. His curiosity flared; he traced the spine as if handling a relic. One passage described an elixir granting the wisdom of a thousand lifetimes---ink made from distilled words.

In the weeks that followed, colleagues noticed his change. His notes turned erratic. He rubbed his temples constantly, laughed a beat too late, and scratched at his forearm as though something writhed beneath the skin.

One mild summer evening, Rachel met Michael leaving the bookstore, arms full of paperbacks.

"Planning another literary feast?" she teased.

"Always," he said. "Seen Dorian lately?"

Not since that night. He's buried in his studies, isn't he?"

"Yes—but what studies?"

They walked beneath the gaslights until Dorian's home came into view. The windows were dark, curtains drawn where once they'd glowed with welcome. Rachel hesitated, then knocked.

Inside, Dorian sat surrounded by open books. The diary lay before him, its pages spread like wings. His fingertips were stained faintly black, as though the ink had seeped beneath his skin.

"Dorian?" Rachel called through the door. "It's us. How about dinner tonight?"

"Not tonight," came a strained reply.

"Come on—you can't resist a good debate."

"You wouldn't understand," he snapped. "You're still just reading the words. I'm becoming them."

Rachel recoiled. "Dorian, what do you mean?"

"You can't help me. You'd never dare walk this path."

"Please," she whispered. "At least open the door."

He didn't. A chair scraped, then silence.

Rachel turned to Michael. "We'll come back tomorrow."

Inside, Dorian exhaled shakily. The diary's whispers curled around his thoughts like smoke. *Just one more passage. Once I gain full knowledge, I'll be unstoppable.* The ink shimmered under lamplight, and the first dark line formed beneath his skin.

Outside, Rachel asked, "What do you think he's found?"

Michael glanced back. "Whatever it is---it's changing him."

***

Dorian raised the quill, the whispers urging him on. The front door, which he'd neglected to lock days before, clicked softly—Rachel and Michael slipped inside after seeing the flare of light in the window.

Dipping the quill into the ink, the liquid shimmered like midnight stars. "I accept," he whispered. "The price for knowledge—not my soul's erasure."

The ink seared as he wrote the final incantation. Black filaments raced beneath his skin like frost on glass. His thoughts spun into chaos. Dark tendrils spread through his veins, a vicious addiction whispering enlightenment while draining his soul. He understood the contract now—power would be granted, but surrender would erase him.

Outside the library, Rachel pressed a hand to the door. "He's in trouble."

Michael whispered, "Tear the source. Name it. Bring light." They had prepared for this—two sleepless nights in the University archives armed them with rites and desperate hope.

Inside, Dorian watched his reflection blur. The shelves seemed to breathe; ink bottles flexed like lungs. Pages fluttered like trapped birds. The mirror reflected a stranger—a creature of shadow and script. The whispers roared.

The library doors banged open.

"Dorian!" Rachel cried.

He turned toward her, eyes burning black.

Michael held up a folded folio. "The diary's the anchor."

Rachel lunged and tore free a fistful of pages. Ink bled across her fingertips like bruised violets. Michael shouted the words they'd memorized; each syllable cracked like thunder.

The room inhaled. Dorian staggered. Rachel yanked the drapes. Sunlight slashed across the floor, striking his hands. The ink recoiled from the light as if scorched.

Silence followed. Dorian collapsed, gasping.

He'd paid the price and survived—not cured, but standing. The whispers ebbed, leaving an aching quiet.

"Dorian, you did it!" Rachel said. Michael steadied his shoulder.

"Don't thank us," Michael said. "You met it halfway so we could pull you back."

"I'm here," Dorian breathed.

That night they drank water instead of wine and spoke little. Laughter came in cautious fragments. Stillness, for once, was enough.

***

"You know, I've never seen a more beautiful sunset than this," Rachel said the next evening, gazing at the copper sky.

"It's been a long time since I've seen one without feeling... tainted," Dorian said.

"It's like the universe threw us a party," Michael added, and the tension broke into laughter.

The following night, Dorian cooked. The dining room smelled of rosemary and wine reduction. Beef Wellington steamed in its crust, ringed by roasted vegetables slick with butter.

Rachel poured sherry while Michael carved. Candles shimmered in crystal stems—a table fit for apology and rebirth.

They spoke of grounding things—campus gossip, rare editions, the cat haunting the quad. The light conversation was a welcome contrast to the darkness that once filled the room.

After dessert—pear tarts with brandy and cream—Rachel leaned back. "I have an idea," she said. "A literary party---a salon, really, where writers and thinkers gather to read, argue, and drink too much sherry. Invite our friends, each room a tribute to an author."

Dorian smiled. "A celebration of stories that survived their darkness."

Ideas flew: the foyer as Poe's parlor with a pendulum centerpiece, the library as Shelley's lab of candles and mirrors, the conservatory for Austen, the cellar for Wells with clockwork curiosities.

Michael grinned. "The mansion's big enough. You still live alone in all this?"

"Always have," Dorian said. "The books keep me company. But lately..." He paused.

"They've been quieter," Rachel said softly.

Her relief was real, though her memory still burned with the image of him writing on his skin while the ink moved beneath the quill. That sound would never leave her.

The night wound down with sherry and laughter.

"To friendship," Dorian toasted.

"To second chapters," Rachel replied.

Thunder murmured beyond the hills. Beneath the library floorboards, the sealed diary slept—or seemed to. A thin line of ink traced the wood grain like a spider's thread.

***

<u>Rachel</u>

The party glittered through every room. The quartet played in the conservatory; Poe's parlor pulsed with feathers and laughter. As the music slowed to a minor key, unease prickled her skin. The clock struck twelve—then twelve again.

<u>Michael</u>

He'd been checking the wards all night. "I hear it," he said. "If the library lights flicker, we move."

Rachel
At the library doors, lamplight pulsed—bright, dim, bright again. "Dorian?" she called.

Dorian
He stood before the mirror where the portrait once hung, watching a thin black line creep along the baseboard. *Not the house*, he thought. *The book.* The curse hadn't died; it had hidden, using the mansion's silence to speak.

Rachel and Michael entered.

"What are you seeing?" Rachel asked.

"Residual ink. The curse binds to readers. The house amplifies it but doesn't create it."

"Then we finish it," she said.

"No bargains. Procedure," Michael said.

They worked as before—Michael angled the mirror, Rachel threw the drapes wide, Dorian named and severed. "Knowledge, yes," Michael said, "but not possession."

The line recoiled, thinned, and dissolved. The clock caught its rhythm again—twelve, then one. The house exhaled.

"You two," Dorian said, "are the difference between wanting power and surviving it."

Later, after the guests left, Michael packed away the mirror.

"For the record," he said, "you never sold your soul. You nearly surrendered to a predatory text."

"Desire opened the door," Dorian said. "We closed it."

"And shoved a chair under it," Rachel added. They laughed, tired but free.

***

Morning brought rain ticking the windows. Dorian joined them at breakfast. "Right as rain," he said, meaning calm, not cure. They planned the salon's next meeting and set new rules: if anything hums, calls, or writes back, they act.

When they left, Dorian checked the library alone. The diary remained sealed, labeled, warded. He locked it again and turned to go—then paused.

A guest's calling card lay on the mantle, gilt edges pristine. A faint black smear curved across the paper, a half glyph in the same hand as the diary. In sunlight, it retreated; in shadow, it darkened, straining to complete itself.

He slid the card into an envelope marked *quarantine*. No panic—just action.

Opening the window, he breathed in the scent of rain and stone. "We keep the lights on," he told the house. "We keep the doors named."

The timbers answered with a slow, contented sigh—alive, but on their side.

The term **Ink Drinker** *comes from the French describing a person who loves to read — one who lives through words rather than merely reading them.*

Supernatural

*The spark for this story came from a search for "descriptive word to describe an avid reader." Of course, my mind went *'Hey! Why don't you take that literally and run with it? It'll be cool.'* It felt cool, until someone in critique pointed out—he didn't drink ink.

The Clicking Never Stops

"You okay?" Sam asked, peering over his newspaper at the new guy, Dave, who had been tapping his chewed-up pencil enough to rattle the stapler.

"Yeah, just... distracted." Dave rubbed his left ear, wincing.

"You've got that look." Sam folded the paper and leaned back. "What's going on?"

Dave hesitated, then leaned in. "I've been hearing this weird noise in my ear. Like faint radio static."

"In both ears?"

"No. Only the left." Dave lowered his voice. "And it's not random. It's like it's... spelling something."

Sam almost laughed, but the look on Dave's face killed the joke in his throat. "You're serious?"

Dave nodded. "It's been days. I can't sleep."

The office fell quiet, the air thick with the hum of lights and the distant clatter of keyboards.

Sam hesitated, then rolled his newspaper into a cone, pressing the narrow end near Dave's ear with an awkward grin. "Hey, just checking..."

But then — he heard it. Faint, rhythmic clicking. Short, long, short. A pattern.

Sam pulled the paper back, his face pale. "No way."

"Morse code," Dave whispered, voice tight. His hands trembled.

***

For years, Dave's tinnitus had been a dull, constant whine—a mosquito trapped behind his eardrum. Doctors called it harmless, a side effect of age, stress, even some hearing loss. He'd accepted it. But two weeks ago, it changed.

The high-pitched hum sharpened into clicks, like an old telegraph machine hammering away. At first, Dave dismissed it as stress, another cruel trick of his overworked brain.

But late one night, as he lay in bed with his pillow pressed tight over his ear, a memory surfaced. His dad, teaching him Morse code as a boy. Enough to tap S-O-S on the table when they were bored.

That's when he realized this wasn't random. This was a message. They started writing the clicks down.

WE ARE WATCHING.

They went online, searching tinnitus forums and obscure message boards, looking for others. They found them: a teacher in Sweden, a retired Marine in Texas, a grad student in Tokyo. All tinnitus sufferers, all hearing the same strange code.

They formed a group, desperate for answers.

Lisa stood out. She was bright, funny, and the first with theories. But one night, she broke.

"I can't do this," she whispered on their video call, eyes red. "I never heard the clicks. I just... wanted to belong."

The group fell silent.

After she signed off, Dave stared at the darkened screen, heart pounding.

Am I dreaming—or losing my mind?

But then the clicks surged again, sharp and insistent.

LISA.

And Dave knew. This was real.

***

The coordinates arrived in a burst of clicks, leading them to a stretch of desert, far from cities and prying eyes.

Under a canopy of stars, they waited.

A light split the sky. The craft descended, sleek, metallic, its surface shimmering with colors that defied description. The hatch opened, and a figure stepped out—humanoid, graceful, its eyes dark as the space between stars.

Its voice spoke straight into their minds.

You are the Chosen. Will you stand with us, or fall silent with your world?

Dave felt his knees shake. His heart hammered. His tinnitus pulsed so hard it rattled his teeth.

He thought of Lisa. Of Sam. Of every sleepless night, every moment, he'd wondered if he was losing his mind.

He stepped forward.

***

The craft's interior defied description—a blend of organic curves and shimmering tech, alive with soft pulses of light. They floated through corridors like veins, led to a central chamber where thin crystalline devices wrapped around their necks.

As the necklaces settled, the tinnitus shifted. The chaotic clicks became a flowing symphony, notes threading into meaning.

Their training began.

They learned to project thoughts, to speak without words. They practiced standing in alien environments, where gravity shifted and light bent.

They walked inside holograms of galactic wars, watched treaties made and broken, learned the fragile weight of diplomacy.

At night, Dave lay in a cocoon-like berth, fists clenched to his ears, the tinnitus louder than ever.

Am I strong enough to save the world or weak enough to fall apart?

The Elyndrans taught, but they did not comfort. The crew had to control fear, doubt, and loss—or fail.

***

When the ship reached its destination, Dave's group stood before an assembly of beings from across the stars.

The Drexxar waited in the shadows, their contempt sharp as knives.

Dave felt the pressure in his skull—the tinnitus, the years of static and pain—crest like a wave.

He stepped forward.

"We come from a world of noise," Dave said, voice rough but steady. "We were drowning in it. Static, division, fear. But through it—" he touched his ear—"we heard you."

"You chose us not because we're perfect, but because we know pain. We know what it's like to carry something you can't silence, can't escape—and still keep going."

His voice grew stronger.

"We are not warriors. We are not conquerors. We are a fractured, beautiful, maddening species that works—every day—to be better."

He looked toward the Drexxar, whose black eyes glittered like obsidian.

"We stand before you as we are: flawed, defiant, human. And we offer not weapons, but understanding."

The air thickened, the fate of Earth—and perhaps the galaxy—hanging in the balance. Amidst the alien voices and the pulsing rhythm of the ship, a single precise note rang out.

A dot. A dash. A pause.

Silence.

The aliens turned toward one another, silent messages flickering across their minds.

The leader of the Drexxar rose, its mouth curving into something almost like a smile—but colder. Its voice cut through the room.

"We concede—for now. We will observe. And we will remember your words."

For a breathless moment, no one moved. Then a ripple passed through the assembly.

Not surrender.

Not victory.

Possibility.

Above them, the Earth turned, wrapped in its hush of clouds and blue. Dave let the tinnitus hum through his skull—a reminder it will never leave. But now, neither will the stars.

###

Psychological Sci-Fi

The spark for this story came from my lifelong tinnitus that recently changed to an annoying clicking in my left ear—sounding like Morse Code.

Beneath the Waves

THE PINKEST FLAMINGO LAWN ornament in Florida stood guard over a puddle of melted ice cream.

Marge wiped her hands on her hibiscus-print muumuu and squinted down the street. "George, honey, our shuttle to the airport is here."

George lowered his crossword. "Airport?" He adjusted his USS Trigger baseball cap, peering past the flamingo. "We're flying somewhere just to get crammed into a sardine can underwater again?"

"Atlantis is in the Bahamas, not down the block," she said, patting his arm. "You promised an adventure for our anniversary."

He grumbled but rose, grabbing the worn leather satchel at his feet—tools inherited from his father, kept oiled and ready for sixty years. "Guess it's too late to suggest miniature golf instead."

Marge's eyes gleamed with the same spark she'd had when they first met—the spark that had talked him into zip-lining in Costa Rica and wandering Moroccan bazaars.

That spark had never led them wrong, only deeper.

Hours later, their small charter plane skimmed over turquoise water toward the Bahamian island of Bimini.

Waiting offshore was their destination: a submersible sleek and blue as a marlin, sunlight flashing off its curved Perspex windows.

Admiring the lush scenery, the passengers gathered dockside.

Friendly chatter and laughter rippled among the strangers, bringing them closer to each other.

Shrieks of delight rang out as children romped in the white sand.

George gestured to a young couple holding hands. "They think it's all fun and games. Wait till we're swimming with the fishes–or become shark bait."

Marge leaned in, eyes sparkling. "You've faced down more sharks than this—*real* ones and the kind behind pool cues."

He groaned.

"Come on, sweetie, you're going to love it."

"If we'd gone to Hawaii like I wanted, we'd be sunburned and happy on the beach."

A booming voice interrupted their banter. "Ahoy, me hearties!" Aloysius "Albatross" Martinelli bellowed. "Today, our destination is the submerged city of Atlantis!"

His crew cheered. Their spirits were as buoyant as the air bubbles rising from the sleek, vibrant-blue submersible bus.

"I modeled this sub-bus after the London double-deckers I loved as a lad. A tour through Stratford-upon-Avon—home of the Bard—lit a fire in me for adventure. Today, I will pass it on to you!"

The sub-bus hatch swung open with a loud metallic groan.

Out stepped a young woman with sea foam-colored eyes and sand-colored hair flashing a sun-bright smile.

Her blue uniform shimmered like the sea, and her name tag read Cap'n Marisol.

"Welcome, adventurers! Next stop—Atlantis!" she called.

"See?" Marge grinned. "A woman after my own heart—full speed ahead."

George sighed, following her aboard. *A casual trip into the abyss. Nothing to worry about.*

The submersible's interior glowed with soft aquamarine light.

Rows of cushioned seats faced panoramic windows where sunlight fractured into golden ribbons.

The hum of the engines was low, hypnotic—like the ocean's own heartbeat.

With a metallic clang, the hatch was sealed. The world above disappeared in a swirl of bubbles and fading light.

Marge reached for George's hand. "You okay, love?"

"Fine," he lied, his voice tight. Confined spaces. Hissing pipes. The smell of oil and metal.

He'd spent enough years under the sea in darker circumstances.

As the submersible descended, the water shifted from turquoise to a darker blue. A voice burst from the speakers: "The Atlantis Adventures welcomes you aboard! I'm your tour guide, Archie."

A little girl clutched her teddy bear.

Kids giggled.

Tourists murmured with anticipation.

"Remember," Archie added, "keep your hands inside. The fish are friendly, but they will envy your snazzy sneakers!"

Laughter rippled through the cabin.

The sub-bus hummed softly as it glided through the ocean, its windows offering a glimpse of the vibrant marine life outside.

Archie stood at the front, a wide grin on his face. Today, he was more than just a tour guide; he was a storyteller, ready to whisk his passengers away to the legendary sunken city of Atlantis.

"I hope you're ready for a journey filled with wonder!" he announced, his voice bright. The passengers—the excited families, curious couples, and a few wide-eyed children—leaned in closer, eager for the tales to begin.

As the sub-bus descended deeper into the ocean, the interior lights cast playful shadows on the walls.

Archie took a deep breath. "Let me tell you about the first time I heard of Atlantis." He paused for effect. "It was from Plato himself—well, not literally. But you get the idea."

Laughter erupted from the group. Archie loved this part.

He painted a picture of Plato, an ancient philosopher, sitting under a tree, scribbling notes about a grand city filled with gold and wisdom.

"Can you imagine? Plato had to convince everyone that Atlantis was real, but who would believe a city just vanished?"

As the sub-bus glided past a school of colorful fish, Archie continued. "Atlantis was said to be a place of harmony, where people lived in peace. They had everything—art, science, and even delicious food! I mean, who wouldn't want to live in a place with endless feasts?"

The passengers chuckled, and one child asked, "What did they eat?"

Archie leaned in, eyes sparkling. "Well, legend says they had giant fruits—grapefruits the size of your head! And fish that could sing!" He mimed a fish dancing in the water, and the children erupted into giggles.

"Now, let's talk about the downfall of Atlantis," he said, tone shifting slightly, but still light. "It wasn't just a simple thing. They became too proud. They thought they were better than everyone else, and that, my friends, is when the gods took action."

He gestured dramatically as the sub-bus turned, revealing an outline of ancient ruins in the distance, cloaked in coral and seaweed.

"And just like that, the city sank to the bottom of the ocean. But don't worry! It's not lost forever. We're on a mission to find it!"

Excitement rippled through the passengers. Archie could see the spark in their eyes, the sense of adventure bubbling under the surface.

He loved these moments—when he could share the magic of history and the thrill of the unknown.

As they neared the ruins, the atmosphere shifted.

The light dimmed, and a sense of wonder filled the space. "Look over there! Those are the remnants of the grand temples," he pointed. "Can you imagine the ceremonies held here, the music that filled the air?"

"Oh, George," Marge whispered, pressing to the glass. "Would you look at that?"

He couldn't help himself; awe crept into his voice. "Guess the brochures didn't lie."

Archie engaged the passengers with questions, urging them to imagine what life may have been like. They shared their thoughts, weaving their own ideas into the fabric of his stories.

"Maybe they held contests!" one girl suggested. "Or had races with sea creatures!"

"Exactly!" Archie beamed. "Atlantis was a place of innovation and creativity. They could have invented the world's first underwater carnival!"

The sub-bus finally came to a halt.

Archie stepped aside, allowing the passengers to peer out of the windows at the enchanting ruins. They were awestruck. T

he remnants of once-grand structures rose like ghosts from the sandy seabed.

"Just think," Archie said softly, "this city was alive once. It thrived with laughter, art, and dreams."

The mood shifted to a reflective wonder. Archie smiled, knowing he had transported them, if only for a moment, into another world.

As they began their journey back, the chatter resumed, now filled with excitement and ideas.

The passengers were no longer just tourists; they were adventurers, explorers of a sunken world, bonded by the stories of Atlantis.

Archie felt fulfilled. He had given them a taste of history and a glimpse of magic.

As the sub-bus began its ascent, he looked out into the ocean, knowing that with every story, Atlantis lived on.

The sub shuddered. George's heart raced as he glanced at Cap'n Marisol. Her expression shifted from curiosity to alarm. "Hold on!" she shouted.

The lights flickered, and Archie's voice turned serious. "Everyone, stay calm!"

With a deafening roar, a creature known as a kraken erupted from the depths. Its tentacles thrashed, slamming against the sub's hull.

Panic laced the air. Then, the lights flickered.

Once. Twice.

The lights flickered again—and died.

A colossal, sucker-studded arm slammed against the glass with a thunderous THOOM. Coffee cups flew.

The sub lurched sideways. Screams erupted.

"Cap'n Marisol, what's happening?" Marge shouted.

Over the speakers came the captain's clipped, fierce voice. "Kraken on our tail! Everyone brace!"

The sub dived sharply.

Metal shrieked as something scraped along its length. George's stomach dropped.

The sound dragged him backward in time—Birmingham, 1943.

Depth charges exploding. A hull groaning like a dying beast.

Water is pouring in. Men shouted prayers that dissolved into bubbles.

He gripped the armrest, eyes wild. *Not again. Not like back then.*

"George!" Marge's voice cut through the noise. "We need you!"

That snapped him out of it. He unbuckled and lunged for the rear hatch. "The compressor failed!" he barked, instincts kicking in. "If we can't expel the ballast water, we won't surface."

He opened the compressor panel. A fuse–blown. He replaced it. Flipped the switch. After sputtering, the compressor roared loudly.

The gauge climbed then stalled. Water refused to drain away.

In the engine bay, he scanned the gauges. Pressure: critically low. He traced the hoses.

A hiss.

Found you. He patched the leak and the water drained. Steam filled the engine room, hot and choking. A pipe near the ballast tanks hissed and sprayed.

George dropped to his knees, wrench already in hand. "Gaff! Anything lever-like!"

A terrified tourist thrust forward a souvenir trident.

"Good enough." George jammed it against the fitting and twisted it. The wrench slipped. Saltwater splattered his face.

The metallic taste hit his tongue, triggering another flash—depth gauge spinning, seawater rising past boots.

He forced the memory down and twisted again, every muscle screaming.

The spray stuttered. Then—stopped.

The alarm went silent. The only sounds were his ragged breathing and the deep thrum of the ocean beyond.

He slumped against the bulkhead, trembling. Marge's face appeared through the crowd, pale but proud.

"Leak contained!" Marisol's voice crackled. "Hold tight—she's taking us up!"

The sub shuddered, engines whining as it climbed. Outside, a tentacle lashed the hull once more, angry but weakening.

Bioluminescent towers of Atlantis flashed below, fading into darkness as they rose.

I survived that, George thought, chest heaving. *I'll survive this.*

As they ascended, George watched jellyfish glide by like parachutes. A shark passed, sleek and silent. A manta ray waved. The pressure eased.

Dark blue gave way to turquoise, then to sunlight.

The submersible burst through the surface in a foamy roar. Waves slapped the glass. Cheers erupted—relief, disbelief, pure human noise.

Seagulls wheeled above as if the ocean itself applauded.

Cap'n Marisol stepped out of the bridge, sweat dampening her temples. "That leak alone would've sunk us in two minutes flat," she said, calm again now. Her gaze flicked to George's USS Trigger cap. "Submarine Service?"

He nodded once.

She offered a crisp nod. "Good work. Coffee's on me."

He chuckled hoarsely. "Make mine decaf. I've had enough adrenaline for one lifetime."

Marge looped her arm through his. "You did it, sailor. And you loved it."

He looked out across the horizon—the sea glittering like a second chance. "Maybe," he said. "But next time..."

He tipped his cap. "...we're going to Hawaii."

Journey to Atlantis, Fantasy/Lore

About the author

TINA HARDEN WRITES STORIES that walk the fine line between beauty and brutality, where humor flickers in the dark and hope survives on stubborn grit. Her second anthology pushes beyond the playful brevity of *From Spark to Story, Vol. 1,* venturing into deeper, more dangerous territory—where love, loss, and resilience meet.

Known for blending humor with heart and a touch of the uncanny, Tina continues to expand her creative range through Soriano Ragazzo Publishing, the imprint she founded to give independent voices a place to shine.

Also by Tina Harden

Short Story Collections

From Spark to Story, Vol. 1 — A collection of short fiction spanning humor, history, and the hauntingly human.
From Spark to Story, Vol. 2 — A collection of longer, grittier tales.
From Spark to Story, Vol. 3 — Longer tales of love, loss, history, and unexpected turns.

Children's Books (Coming Soon)

Cameron and Tigger the Tabby Series — A delightful series following two curious friends whose mischief always leads to heart.

More From Spark to Story stories